THE PLAYER KING

SOME OTHER
HISTORICAL NOVELS
BY AVI

THE PLAYER
KING

AVI

A RICHARD JACKSON BOOK

ATHENEUM BOOKS FOR YOUNG READERS
atheneum   New York   London   Toronto   Sydney   New Delhi

𝒜 ATHENEUM BOOKS FOR YOUNG READERS
atheneum

An imprint of Simon & Schuster Children's Publishing Division

1230 Avenue of the Americas, New York, New York 10020

This book is a work of fiction. Any references to historical events, real people, or real places are used fictitiously. Other names, characters, places, and events are products of the author's imagination, and any resemblance to actual events or places or persons, living or dead, is entirely coincidental.

Text copyright © 2017 by Avi Wortis Inc.

Cover illustration copyright © 2017 by Shane Rebenschied

All rights reserved, including the right of reproduction in whole or in part in any form.

ATHENEUM BOOKS FOR YOUNG READERS is a registered trademark of Simon & Schuster, Inc. Atheneum logo is a trademark of Simon & Schuster, Inc.

For information about special discounts for bulk purchases, please contact Simon & Schuster Special Sales at 1-866-506-1949 or business@simonandschuster.com.

The Simon & Schuster Speakers Bureau can bring authors to your live event. For more information or to book an event, contact the Simon & Schuster Speakers Bureau at 1-866-248-3049 or visit our website at www.simonspeakers.com.

Also available in an Atheneum Books for Young Readers hardcover edition

Book design by Debra Sfetsios-Conover and Irene Metaxatos

The text for this book was set in Goudy Oldstyle.

Manufactured in the United States of America   0918 OFF

First Atheneum Books for Young Readers paperback edition October 2018

10 9 8 7 6 5 4 3 2 1

The Library of Congress has cataloged the hardcover edition as follows:

Names: Avi, 1937- author.

Title: The player king / Avi.

Description: First edition. | New York : Atheneum Books for Young Readers, 2017. | "A Richard Jackson Book." | Summary: In 1486 England, a penniless kitchen boy named Lambert Simnel is told by a mysterious friar that he, Lambert, is actually Prince Edward, the true King of England, setting him on a dangerous course to regain the throne. Based on a true story.

Identifiers: LCCN 2016042037

ISBN 9781481437684 (hardback) | ISBN 9781481437691 (paperback)

ISBN 9781481437707 (eBook)

Subjects: LCSH: Simnel, Lambert—Juvenile fiction. | CYAC: Simnel, Lambert—Fiction. | Kings, queens, rulers, etc.—Fiction. | Great Britain—History—Tudors, 1485-1603—Fiction. | BISAC: JUVENILE FICTION / Historical / Europe. | JUVENILE FICTION / Action & Adventure / General. | JUVENILE FICTION / Royalty.

Classification: LCC PZ7.A953 Pm 2017 | DDC [Fic]—dc23 LC record available at https://lccn.loc.gov/2016042037

FOR JACK,
MY FELLOW WRITER

OXFORD, ENGLAND
1486

Though I am but a kitchen boy,
wondrous things happened to me.
All of it is true.

ONE

MY TALE BEGINS in Oxford, England, in the Year of our Lord 1486. At the time, I was living, sleeping, and forever working in a place known as Tackley's Tavern on the High Street. The tavern was a deep, cellar place, darkful, foul, and loud-tongued so that of all the never-ending chores I was required to do, the one task I truly liked was going out to fetch the bread. Only then did I gain a bit of daylight liberty.

When I went walking out that morning, a rare, bright sun was over loft. It had rained the night before, so the city stench was but slight. The High Street was crowded with children, women, and men, plus dogs and pigs. There were scholars, beggars, clerics, soldiers, and merchants, including wealthy folk in their finery. The clothing most wore was far better than my own tattered brown tunic, and their feet were wrapped in leather, not mud as were mine. A goodly number of people were even clean. As for the dog and pigs, they, like me, were mostly skin and bones, all slubberly with soot.

The street was lined by three-story timbered houses that leaned over my head while all kinds of pretty flags fluttered. Painted and carved signs proclaimed what was being sold in shops. Keepers of stalls were crying, "New onions!" "Spices!" "Meat pies!"

Being always hungry, I would have much loved to have devoured a round dozen pies. Alas, I possessed not so much as a farthing, the smallest coin in the kingdom—one fourth of a penny.

It was as I passed before All Saints Church that I heard the swirl of pipe and beating drum. Observing that a crowd had gathered, I was curious to learn the reason why. I was always wishing to enjoy a free pastime, so I wiggled to the front.

To my great delight, what I saw was a band of

players about to perform an interlude on a rickety platform before a frayed cloth. The cloth, hanging from a rope, bore a painting of a castle. Musicians stood on either side of the platform, one playing a recorder, the other thumping a tabor. A woman held up a banner with words, which no doubt explained what story was to be mimed. It mattered nothing to me that I could not read: Street interludes were usually full of jolly sport and I loved them.

Three players—all men—strode out from behind the painted cloth. They wore motley costumes, multi-patched and many colored. One man had a black beard tied to his chin, and a crumped crown—something colored gold—on his head. I guessed he was meant to be a king.

In one hand, this player king dangled a live piglet—a blue ribbon tied round its head—which squealed and twisted about in great distress. In the king's other hand was a large sword made of wood.

Just to see it all made me grin.

Two other players, dressed as women, knelt before the king and held up their hands, as if begging.

"Oh, great King Solomon," one of them cried in a

loud, high-pitched voice. "That sweet babe is mine!"

No sooner did "she" say this than the piglet let out an unruly squeal. That sent the crowd into loud laughter, in which I joined.

Then the other pretend woman cried, "Not true, beloved King. It is *my* beautiful child!"

The piglet gave yet another scritching scream, which pleased the crowd even more. My empty stomach hurt with laughing.

In a loud voice, the player king proclaimed, "Since I am the great king Solomon, full of noble wisdom, it is for me to decide to which of you this child belongs. Since you both say this babe is yours, I shall cut him in twain, so each may have half." He lifted his sword.

"Yes," said one of the women, "that's the wisest thing to do."

"No! No!" cried the other woman. "Don't do that, O great King. Let the child live whole with her, rather than cut him in two."

"Aha!" said the king. "Surely true love always champions life. Thus, a woman who does *not* wish the child to die must be the real mother. I say, let *her* have it."

With that, he handed the piglet to the woman, who caused the beast to squeak and wrenk so much it broke free, and the king and two women had to scuddle madly to catch it.

This prompted the crowd to the greatest crowing of all, in which I joined with utmost glee.

These players retired behind the castle cloth, but two others came forth, including yet another who was meant, I think, to be God the Father, because a halo was fastened to his head and a white beard was tied to his chin. Another man—called Noah—held a goblet and acted drunk. Though God warned him a great flood would come unless he stopped drinking, this Noah drank anyway, so God dumped a filled piss-pot over him. The crowd roared.

Oh, how I adored such jests.

Finally, two men came forward and began to do a jig as the musicians played. The most nimble was the player king. The other players—in their costumes—walked about with hats, begging for coins.

The interlude over, I pushed through the crowd intent upon going on to the bakery. The comedy had filled me with joy.

It was only when I stepped back into the High

Street that I realized a friar had followed me and now stood staring after me. I recognized him as a Dominican priest, of the order known as Black Friars because they wore black cloaks over white robes.

He was a tall, sinewy man, his pate shaved on top, tonsure style. He had a smooth, narrow-headed, and sharp-chinned face, piercing eyes, a long nose, and small, somewhat pointy ears. Pale hands, which emerged from his black cloak, were clasped piously over his robes, while his delicate fingers suggested he pushed pens, not plows. On his slender feet he wore sandals.

I recalled having seen this priest at Tackley's Tavern any number of times. He always made me think of a sleek hunter's hound. But this time, the way he stood there looking at me suggested *I* was a rabbit, which he had a mind to catch, cook, and eat.

Refusing to have him dull my spirits, I gave him no further heed and continued on to the bakery. But I shall tell you true: If this priest had never seen me, my life would have been very different.

TWO

HAVING GONE TO the bakery, I walked back to Tackley's, carrying a full basket and chewing a crust of bread. As I did, I kept thinking about the interlude, and how grand it would be to wander about the country being a player king so as to make people bow down to me. What fun to make folk laugh. How much pleasure it would give me to make my master, Einar Tackley, squeal like the pig he was!

I truly gave some thought to joining the players, but reminded myself that running away from one's master was a hanging offense. Yet I hasten to assure you, if I *had* been hanged, no one would have cared.

In truth, I knew perfectly well that my life was worth little more than a flout, which is to say a *mocking* laugh, not merry, but mean. My every waking moment—save when I went to the bakery—was spent receiving kicks, cuffs, and curses. Oxford's street dogs were better treated than I.

Consider my name, Lambert Simnel. No one—and that included me—had any notion how I got it: Did *they*, whoever who named me, mean it to be odd? It didn't matter; Lambert Simnel *is* what people called me.

I might have been nine, ten, or even thirteen years of age. I wasn't sure.

Yes, I lived in Oxford, but had no idea how I'd gotten there. No more than I knew where I'd been born or anything about my parents.

Did I have brothers, sisters, uncles, or cousins? I couldn't have said.

As to height, I believed I was four, maybe four and a half feet tall, but in those days I could neither count nor measure.

The words I most often heard were, "Do as you're told!" And you may be very sure I hastened to do exactly that, since I was an orphan kitchen boy, sneered at as a base scullion.

You will understand then why my time consisted of trying to lap up every lick of life I could, though what I lapped was very little. Indeed, since each day was the same as the one before, I had no doubt that my next day—assuming I lived to see it—would be just the same. In short, my life was worth no more than a spot of dry spit.

THREE

I RETURNED to Tackley's Tavern. Being a cellar space, it had no windows, just candle lamps to poke some little light into darkful corners. The air there was forever fogged and fumy from the hearth fire, which burned dawn to dawn. It was here I truly lived.

There were trestle tables set about with benches to serve patrons. For farthings and pennies you could buy food and drink. I managed to stay alive by eating table-leavings, and now and then some crusts of bread.

At night, I slept on the hard, rush-strewn dirt floor.

The customers at Tackley's were peasants, yeomen, shopkeepers, traders, civil clerks, and university students. Jibes and japes were the common talk, the cruder the better.

High-class people were not welcome at Tackley's. If, by some mishap, they tripped down our steps, they were slapped with slurs and sped away.

With so many friaries and monasteries in Oxford, priests and friars also came to Tackley's. Usually, they kept to the tavern's night-like niches, dipping into their drinks like dabbing ducks, dreariheaded for having been slighted by someone higher. Still, I was told I must always show respect to any cleric who appeared, even if they had drowned in their cups.

That morning, when I came down the steps hauling the basket of bread, Mistress Tackley, who was as big, round, and loud as a cathedral bell, demanded to know what had taken me so long.

"I went on a pilgrimage to Canterbury," I said, which caused her to pull my hair, call me a sluggish skellum, and predict a quick hanging.

I gave her the bread and hastened to my work, calling over my shoulder, "You deep patch of dung!"

She shook a fist at me but I didn't care. Insults and threats were what we shared. I went back to work.

Of all my tasks, the most important was cooking mutton. Before an open fire, I had to slather the mutton with butter, dredge the chunks with salt and flour, spear them on a spit, and constantly turn that spit so as to roast the meat. While spinning the spit, I had to catch hot fat in the dripping pan, baste the mutton with those sizzling sauces, and know the moment it would melt—to be sure, not in *my* mouth but my master's.

I don't know how long I'd been turning the spit when I noticed that the friar, the very same Dominican priest who was at the interlude staring after me, was now standing in the smoky haze at the bottom of our steps.

He stood there and studied me for some long, gawping moments. This time, however, as if making up his mind, he drew close, leaned in, and whispered, "Boy, I know who you really are."

I looked about, assuming the friar was talking to someone else. Not finding anyone near, I turned back around. "Sir Priest," said I, "who are you talking to?"

"I said I know who you are." His voice was low.

Perplexed, I looked at him and said, "I assure you, Brother, I'm only Master Tackley's kitchen boy."

He moved closer and fairly hissed, "What do you call yourself?"

"Lambert Simnel," I said, and edged away.

The friar made a soothing smile. "Named, I trust, after Saint Lambert who preached to the pagans."

Since all kinds of odd folks came to Tackley's, I decided it best if I just humored the priest. "Truly, Brother, I'm no saint and I've never met a pagan I liked."

"Don't jest with me," he snapped. "Who is your father?"

"Don't know."

"Mother?"

"I ran off before we were introduced."

"An orphan, then?"

"My parents have always avoided me."

"How old are you?"

Irritated by his persistent questions, I just shrugged.

"How did you come to be here?"

"Some bad storm blew me in."

"But you must have come from *somewhere*."

I was becoming exasperated. "Please, Brother, I've chores to do. Talk to Master Tackley. He's the one who keeps me and has done so for my whole life."

"*Whole* life?"

"God willing, it's not over yet."

"I will speak to him," said the friar, but instead he edged even closer so that I could smell his clove-scented breath. "Boy, do you know the king of England? Know his name? When he came to the throne? *How* he came to it?"

Increasingly irked, I said, "Forgive me. Kings or princes don't speak to me."

"Ah!" cried the friar. "The two murdered princes. Perhaps you know about *them*."

Not liking talk of murder, I tried to move away.

He followed, edging me into a corner. "What about the Earl of Warwick?" he demanded, his voice full of urgency.

"Earls? I only know about the *eels* we serve in spring. Good eating."

"You say you know nothing about Warwick?"

"Warwicks or candlewicks?"

"There's a rumor," the friar pressed, "that Warwick escaped his imprisonment in the London Tower. Do you know anything about *that*? Where he's hiding?"

"Believe me," I cried, altogether infuriated, "if there's news to know, I'm the last to learn it."

"I am not deceived," the brother said. "I know what you are doing."

With that, he turned his back on me and walked away, leaving me quite baffled.

FOUR

I WATCHED THE friar stride to where Master Tackley stood at the back of the tavern, pouring drink into cups and bowls.

This master of mine, Einar Tackley, husband of Mistress Tackley, was a bald, fleshy man of middling years. He not only owned the tavern, but brewed the drink. Looking like a large pig, he had a face to match and a neck so wide it was no neck at all. His speech was as foul as a trish-trash ditch and his fists heavy as hammers, which he was more than happy to pound on me.

He and the friar talked, their glances now and

again slinking toward me. Praying I was not in trouble, I tried to hear, but there was too much clitter-clatter in the air for me to catch any of their words.

When their conversation stopped, the brother withdrew into shadows, but kept watching me. I went back to my fire, pretending to ignore him. When he finally quit the tavern, I was relieved. Thinking him outlandish, I wanted nothing to do with him.

No sooner had he gone, however, than Master Tackley lumbered over and looked down at me with his wet, pink eyes as if trying to see me in a new way.

"Boy!" he said. "What did that Black Friar say to you?"

Wearied by all these pointless questions, I said, "He thinks I'm a fool for working here."

"Tell me what he said!"

"He claimed to know who I was, Master."

"What did you tell him?"

This being the kind of banter I was used to, I replied, "That I was a rich merchant on my way to Bartholomew Fair."

"Don't trifle with me!" cried Tackley, lifting a fist.

I backed away. "He asked me, sir, if the king of England was my friend."

"What did you say?"

"I told the truth. No one of quality ever visits Master Tackley's tavern."

Tackley lashed out with his thick fist, but having sensed he would do exactly that, I ducked under his arm, dashed into the busiest part of the cellar, and leaped upon a crowded table. "Oh, help me!" I cried in mockery. "My master is about to slay me!"

"Fight! Fight!" came a chorus of cheers and jeers from the patrons.

Master Tackley, his face as ruddy as the reddest rose, stormed over to the table. "Want-wit!" he roared. "Mudsill! Boiled bootlicker! Get down!" He kept trying to grab me with his massy hands.

Dancing about the table beyond his reach, I jeered, "You old gundy-gut! Come and get me!"

The boisterous patrons began to bang their tankards on the tables. "Fetch him, Tackley! Slap the boy down! Break the baby's bones!" A shower of bread bits, drink, and meat were flung at me.

Furious, Tackley tried to climb the table, but his

clumsy bulk made him fall on his bum. The uproar grew greater.

Tackley hauled himself up, glared at me for a moment, then abruptly yelled, "Never mind! I'll spill no sweat on someone who's a splat of spittle on my left boot's heel. Don't think you're anything, boy. You've got no kin. No brains. You're a nobody!" he fairly shouted. "Do you hear me, boy? A *nobody*!" With that he turned his back on me and lumbered off.

Tackley's furious screeches silenced the inn, but every eye in the room was upon me left standing alone on the table. As I stood there, a sense of my nothingness filled me with deep shame.

My eyes tearing, I somehow managed to climb down, and slunk back to my work, trying to act as if my heart felt no pain. Not so. I vowed I'd have my own on Tackley.

Except I had no idea how I could do it.

FIVE

LATE AT NIGHT the same day, and outside, a steady rain was bucketing, the water trickling down our stone steps and seeping over the floor, turning it to mud. Candles were all but gutted, so only little light lingered. In the tavern's dullest corners a few cup-shot men slumbered. Though my yawns were bigger than my head, I was still at cleaning chores when the Black Friar came down the steps.

His bald pate was glistening wet, his black cloak dripped. In the demi-dark his face seemed as white as a ghost. A manservant was with him, holding up a flaming torch.

When the brother reached the bottom, he paused and looked about, only to fasten his eyes on me. Though unhappy to see him, I acted as if I didn't notice. All the same he approached and said, "Where's your master?"

"Back room, I think, Brother."

"Fetch him."

When I hesitated, the friar said, "Do as you're told."

Reluctantly, uneasy he was there, I went to my master's back room, a small, ill-lit place, stinking of sweat and dregs. It had a wide straw-stuffed bed and an old cleft table upon which a burning candle was stuck in a pool of gray wax. On the floor was Tackley's iron-strapped money chest. It was open.

My master sat at the table, his wife across. Before him lay the day's earnings: a meek mound of farthings, groats, and pennies. Beneath Mistress Tackley's greedy gaze, the tavern keeper was tallying the coins with his fat, dirty fingers.

"Master," I whispered, "that Black Friar is back."

Tackley stopped counting. "What does he want?"

"You."

Master and Mistress eyed one another. If they

said anything, I didn't hear. The next moment, Tackley—with a grunt—heaved himself up from the table.

When he stepped to the door I started to follow. He shoved me back. "Stay here and make sure she doesn't steal anything." He pointed to his wife and went out.

Moments later Tackley returned with a leather pouch. He pitched it onto the table, where it landed with a *clink*, the unmistakable sound of coins.

His wife glanced up.

"He purchased the boy," Tackley announced to her. Only then did he turn to me. "Go to the friar. He's your new master."

"Sir . . . ?" I gasped, not sure I'd heard correctly.

"Are you *deaf*, boy? The priest bought you. You're his."

I stood there, astonished.

"Go!" cried Tackley.

I was too frightened to move.

"Didn't you hear?" Tackley bellowed. "You belong to him. Leave!"

"Did . . . did you know he was coming back for me?" I asked.

"Out!" shouted Tackley.

Speechless, confused, unable to grasp how my life could wrinkle so quickly, I remained in place until Tackley raised a fist, ready to strike.

Unwillingly, I crept back to the main room. The Black Friar stood there, looking down at me as if to assay his purchase. The manservant was on the steps.

Trembling, I peeked up, my head a-tumble with questions. *What is going to happen? I've never been anywhere else. How can I leave Tackley's? How will this priest use me?*

"Come along."

I looked to see if I could run away, but the manservant blocked the only escape.

I glanced back. Master Tackley stood watching. I gave him a pleading look. He ignored it.

Full of dread but having no choice, I followed the friar out of the tavern.

SIX

HEAVY RAIN WAS falling from the dark sky.

"Follow me," said the priest.

Instantly drenched, heart thumping, I found tongue to ask, "Please, Sir Priest, where are we going?"

"To the friary where you will become what you truly are."

"What . . . what is that?"

He scowled and for a moment I thought he might answer, but with a sharp glance at the servant—as if to say "not with him around"—he only said, "In time," turned, and started down the puddled, muddy street.

I took a step so as to bolt away, only to have the servant snatch my arm to keep me from going.

We started walking.

"Brother," I called as we went along, my bare feet squissing in the mud, "might I know your name?"

"Brother Richard Simonds," was his reply—to which he added, "No more talk."

His long strides forced me to take half skips to keep up. There was pain in my stomach. I was trembling. Feeling as if I were following a shadow, I kept my eyes on the friar's black cloak. *What's going to happen to me?* I kept thinking.

The manservant, hard upon my back, kept poking me on.

Church bells tolled the late hour. I decided the friar had chosen the time so no one would see what was happening. The thought thickened my fright.

The rain poured down. We hurried along the High Street, passing All Saints Church, which made me think of the players. How I wished then I'd gone over to them. I considered bolting again, but the servant, as if guessing my thoughts, gripped me harder. I couldn't break free.

At St. Martin's Church we turned and proceeded along Fish Street, crossed Trill Stream, and then made another turn, going by the mill. I tried to keep our passage in mind so—when I had the chance—I could run back to Tackley's.

Before us loomed the fortress-like Dominican friary with its high square tower. The brother approached a small wooden door—strap hinged and studded with rusty iron nails. He was not, I realized, using the main entrance. All he did increased my dismay. *Why such secrecy?*

The brother yanked the door open, gestured for me to enter, and stepped inside. With the servant pushing me, I stumbled in. The door slammed behind me.

Fearful as to what might happen next, I peered about. We were at the head of a deserted hall. A few lanterns revealed rows of slender pillars extending into murkiness. Though I saw no other people, I heard the sound of sacred singing, slow and sorrowful, as if from another sphere.

Is he going to kill me?

The friar handed the servant a groat, and in

return the man gave him his torch and went away. I never saw him again.

"Brother—"

"No talk," the friar said softly. "Move along. I'm right behind you."

He forced me to descend steep stone steps, so narrow I had to press my hands upon the frigid walls on either side to keep from falling. Once below, we came upon a cave-like passageway with brown walls and many doors. Using a large key, the priest opened one of them.

His light revealed a small monk's cell with white walls. A plain wooden crucifix hung upon one wall, under that was a praying stool. Near another wall lay a squared pile of straw, which I took to be a bed. A small table and stool. Nothing else, not even a window.

The friar gestured to the straw. "Say your prayers and go to sleep," he said.

"Please, sir, I beg you to tell me—"

"Not now," he said.

Taking the torch with him, he left, slamming the door behind him. All was dark. I know the door was locked because I felt for it, tried to open it, banging, kicking, and calling. To no avail.

Cold, wet, and shivery, I was a prisoner. I knew not why. Only one thought filled my head: *What is going to happen to me?*

SEVEN

I DON'T KNOW the hour when the friar, candle in hand, woke me. I sat up, rubbed my face, and looked about, forgetting for the moment all that had happened. When I remembered, all my distress returned.

The priest's candlelight allowed me to see that he had placed some bread and cheese, as well as a jug, on the small table. The smell of food stirred me. The bread, however, was white, not dark barley-oat bread, my normal fare. Since I had never been allowed to eat white bread, I merely looked at it, my mouth watering.

Brother Simonds gestured. "Go on," he said. "Eat."

"Truly?" I asked.

"Of course."

Before the friar could change his mind, I stuffed my mouth as if pushing a cork into a bottle. When he told me I might eat the cheese too, I did. While I bolted the food, and drank, he watched me intently, as if my eating could tell him things.

When I'd done, he said, "You'll remain here. I don't wish you to be seen on the streets."

I flung myself on my knees and lifted my hands in supplication. "Please, Sir Priest, I swear by all the saints and each and every holy martyr, if you believe I'm someone else, you're wrong. I'm a nobody. Ask Master Tackley."

"I don't care what you say," he said. "I know who you are."

"Who?" I asked, as baffled as ever.

Instead of answering, he took his candle and left, leaving me in that dark cell. I tried to open the door. It was useless.

I remained in the darkness, longing to be back at Tackley's Tavern: turning the spit, dodging blows and insults, doing whatever Master ordered me to do. That was the world I knew. Moreover, since the tavern was rarely quiet, the silence surrounding me now was frightening. All I could hear was my own fear.

EIGHT

AFTER WHAT SEEMED forever, the friar returned. This time he brought a clerical robe, such as he wore, but sized for me.

"Put this on. And cover your face."

"Why?"

"You must not be seen."

Puzzled, I looked up at him. "Brother, there's no one else here to see me but you."

"We are going out."

"Where?"

"You'll learn when you get there."

I pulled the thick wool robe over my tunic—glad,

at least, for the warmth. He fixed the cowl so my face was mostly hidden.

"Now come," he said. "No talk."

We stepped outside. It was evening, so I knew a whole day had passed. Though the rain had ceased, the air was curded with mist, which swirled like a low, damp cloud. The world seemed to have lost its shape. Not knowing where we were going or why, my anxiety fairly gnawed on my heart.

Clutching me tightly with one hand, the friar used his hooded lamp to guide us silently through narrow, crooked ways. He was avoiding the main streets. It was clear to me that whatever the brother intended, he wished it secret. You might not think it possible for my fright to increase, but it did.

I decided that the best way of escaping would be by asking strangers for help, claiming I was being stolen. But every time someone emerged out of the mist, the friar shoved me to one side, slapped a hand across my mouth, and stood over me. I couldn't speak or get away.

It was only when we came into the Queen's College area that he halted.

"We're going there." He gestured toward a huge

building with light blooming from its many windows.

"What is that place?" I asked, eyeing the building warily.

By way of answering, Brother Simonds turned me around and forced me to look up at him, holding his lamp so close to my face I felt its heat. His own face, peering out from his hood, was, to my surprise, full of unease.

"Is there some danger here?" I managed to whisper.

Squeezing me painfully by my shoulders, he said, "Speak only when you are spoken to. If you are told to do something, do it."

"What is it? What's going to happen?"

"You're going to stand before a noble person."

"Who?"

"You'll learn soon enough."

"Why would such a person want me?"

"He needs you."

"*Needs?*"

The friar's grip grew tighter, his face more intense. "Just know that how you act will determine if you live."

"Am I going to die?" I cried.

"You'll do as you're told. Now, be still."

The brother led me—heart thumping, legs weak—into the building by way of an open court where horses with rich trappings were tied. We passed under a kind of porch, and then went through heavy doors into an enormous hall. Four soldiers with armor, helmets, and swords stood on guard. *Are they*, I wondered, *to be my executioners?*

I looked about. Many people, mostly men but some women, were milling about. All were finely garbed.

As for the room, the ceiling was high, with vaulting beams. Some kind of wheel was hanging down, on which lit candles had been placed. Bright lanterns were set about. Armor, flags, swords, shields, and lances were on the walls, while sweet incense perfumed the air. I also noticed a gigantic fireplace. Five fireplaces such as existed in Tackley's could have fit within this one, in which huge logs were burning. The room was very warm. All in all, the hall displayed more wealth and power than I had ever seen before. *Why am I here?* I kept asking myself.

The friar bent over and whispered, "Keep your hood low."

I did as told but managed to peek out. At the furthest end of the room, opposite from where we stood, was a raised platform and a long table. Behind that table, in the middle, was a large padded chair. Smaller chairs were ranged to either side.

Seated in the largest chair was a young man. He was wearing a black velvet cap, a black tunic with slashed sleeves showing scarlet, and a ruffed white collar. Jeweled rings gleamed on his fingers.

His hair was close-cropped and he had a well-trimmed, if thin, beard of ruddy hue that came to a short point. His eyes were large, dark, and, so it seemed to me, full of anger. His thin lips suggested cruelty.

All around were courtiers waiting on him. These people approached, bowed, offered up plates of food, drink, or what looked to be sheets of parchment. Some of these offerings the young man took. Others he brushed away with a scornful wave of his hand.

Taking an instant dislike to the man, I tugged on Brother Simonds's robe. "Who *is* that?" I asked, my voice low.

Into my ear the friar said, "He's the Earl of Lincoln.

John de la Pole, cousin to a queen. Nephew of King Richard. Head of the house of York. England's most powerful Lancastrian lord."

Quite astonished, I said, "Is *he* the one who needs me?"

"Shhh!" the friar cautioned, his face tight with strain. It made me think that it wasn't just me who was about to be judged fit to live or die, but him, too.

The Earl of Lincoln glanced up. His eyes made a sweep across the hall, only to halt when he saw the friar and me. The hardness of his look deepened my dread.

Next moment, Lincoln sat back in his chair and made a motion with his hand. An old white-bearded man, robed in black and yellow silks, with a chain of what looked like gold round his neck, stood up. Lincoln said something to him, after which the old man faced the room and clapped his hands. "The earl," he called, "requires all of you to withdraw. Brother Simonds will remain."

There was much bowing, backing, and leaving, with many a questioning glance at the friar, but happily, not me.

Within moments, even the soldiers had retreated. Only three people remained in that huge hall: the Earl of Lincoln, the friar, and me, Lambert Simnel. I felt very small. The beating of my heart seemed very large. I had come, I had no doubt, to learn my fate.

NINE

THE FRIAR PEELED away the cowl that covered my head.

Lincoln stared at me with intense curiosity. "Is *this* the boy you told me about?" he called across the room to Brother Simonds.

"He is, my lord."

"And *where* did you find him?"

"Here in Oxford, my lord. Working in a tavern."

Lincoln continued to gaze at me. "Come here," he barked.

I was too scared to move. The friar had to push me.

Hardly daring to breathe, fearful of drawing too close, I edged forward, then stopped and peeked up.

Lincoln remained sitting, fingers drumming the tabletop, eyes fixed on me. "Nearer!" he cried, his voice whip-like.

Trembling, I did as told.

"Halt!"

I stopped.

Lincoln rubbed his beard. His eyes aimed at me like sharp spear points. He bit the side of his thumb. As if agitated, the fingers of his left hand continued to tap the table. I tried to guess his thoughts—how he considered me. I could not.

Abruptly, he stood, came out from behind his table, and walked about me much the way I had seen Master Tackley judge a sheep he was offered for slaughter.

"Is he well-witted?" Lincoln called out.

"He is, my lord," said the friar.

Well-witted! No one had ever attached that word to me before.

"Is he reasonable? Follows orders?"

"My lord, he'll do what he's told."

That, at least, was what everybody asked of me.

"Remove his robe," Lincoln commanded.

The friar pulled off my clerical gown, so that I stood in my tattered tunic, bare feet, and normal dirt. I felt ashamed, a loathed nobody, just the way I was when standing on the table at Tackley's Tavern. I felt nothing but contempt for myself.

The earl reached out and gripped my chin, his rings painfully pricking my skin. To study my face he turned my head this way and that, the way traders considered horses.

"Where do you come from?" he asked.

Seeking some notion how to reply, I tried to shift toward Brother Simonds.

Lincoln held me fast. "Look at *me!*" he snapped, jerking my chin up. "Now, again, where do you come from?"

"Master Tackley's tavern, my lord."

"No. *Before!*" He was holding my face so tightly I felt like crying out.

"I don't know, my lord," I whispered.

"Louder!"

"Please, I don't know where I'm from."

"No idea?"

The friar called out, "People say he's an orphan."

"What name do you use?"

"Lambert Simnel, my lord."

"Is that what he's called?" Lincoln asked the friar.

"Does it matter, my lord?"

The earl released me and wiped his hand on his tunic as if he had touched slime. "Walk about," he said.

Though hating it, I did as told.

"Enough!"

I stopped.

The next moment Lincoln cried, "He's dirty!" and turned his back on me as something despicable. Though I had no idea what had happened, I felt that deep shame again.

"My lord," said the friar, "he will be mucked." He dropped the robe over me as if capping a candle.

To Brother Simonds, Lincoln said, "But you believe you can . . . bring back this boy's memory and manners?"

"All that's needed, my lord, is money, and a place to work."

"Done secretly?"

"You and I, my lord, have discussed the consequence if otherwise."

Lincoln considered me with his hard eyes. "Very well," he said to the friar. "You shall have the money. For a while anyway. But in God's name, clean him. I can't abide filth. And feed him! He must look smooth."

Ten

ORDERED INTO a corner while the friar and Lincoln conferred, I tried to listen, but heard nothing. I tried to guess what was happening but couldn't. Then I saw the earl give the friar a purse and key, and a tremor passed through me, fearful that I had been sold again. Instead the brother returned to me and said, "Come along. But cover your face and stay close."

We passed out of the hall, even as those who had stood attendance on the earl flowed back in. Not understanding what had happened, I didn't know if I should feel relieved or more alarmed.

As soon as the friar and I were alone a
on the dark streets, I said, "Sir Priest, I don't
that lord likes me. What does he want of me? I'm
nothing."

"I assure you, he wants what's best for you."

"What's that?"

"He knows who you are and wants to return you
to your proper station."

I halted. "I beg you, Brother. Just tell me who he
thinks I am."

"You'll remember soon enough."

"Why can't you tell me now? You told him I was
well-witted."

"You are well-witted."

I decided it would be best to play the jester.
"Please, sir," I said, "Why do you say that?"

The friar abruptly halted, clutched the robe about
my neck, and put his face close to mine. "Just do as
you're told!" he said, and gave me a shove forward.

As we continued on through back streets, it
didn't take long for me to realize we were not walking toward to the friary. We were going somewhere
else. I was afraid to ask where.

At last we came to a stop. Brother Simonds's

see a timbered house of
ilding at a corner plot. Its
eams, were filled with clay,
The roof was thatched. All
ke the earl's home. Rather,
rdinary house, except I had
never been in ... ly life, may I remind you, had
been spent in a cellar, like a rotten turnip.

The friar unlocked the door. We stepped into an open space with a few boxes, barrels, and casks standing about in no particular order. I took it for a storage place, a place of business.

I said, "Who lives here?"

"You."

"*Me?*"

"The building belongs to Lincoln. He ordered the people to leave."

"Why?"

"So you might be kept here."

"Will I be locked up?" I cried.

"Of course not. I'll be here."

I waited for more explanation, but the friar only took care to secure the door behind us and stow the key in his cloak. Then he led the way up the steps to the second level, the solar, which was a large room containing a bed, table, chairs, chests, and open larders. The larders were empty, but there were usable candles on the table.

"Here's where we shall live and work."

"What kind of work?"

His answer was to light two candles. Then he pointed to the chair and said, "Sit down."

I eyed him with apprehension but did as bid, wiped my nose with my dirty fingers, and waited tensely for I knew not what.

Brother Simonds stood before me, eyes fixed on my face. His pale hands were clasped, his body tense. Behind him, his narrow shadow loomed high like an immense church gargoyle.

"Now, then," he said, "I am going to tell you who you are."

ELEVEN

"PLEASE, SIR; I'm Lambert Simnel, the kitchen boy. A nobody scullion."

"Be still!" the friar snapped. Though it was cool, the friar's face glistened with sweat. His eyes shone unnaturally bright as if stirred by what he was about to say. His breathing was quick, agitated. "Now, listen with care."

I waited, not knowing what I was waiting for.

The priest began to talk. It was about things of which I knew nothing, matters as remote as the moon. All about English kings, who, despite their greatness, must have had small imaginations, for they were forever named Edward, Richard, or Henry.

He spoke much of King Edward the Third, who lived many years ago. He talked of children, cousins, marriages, rivalries and sudden deaths, persons who claimed the throne, and those who didn't. He mentioned earls, barons, dukes, and queens, as well as a mad king named Henry the Sixth.

The names and deeds of these mingled and oft times mangled monarchs, their lofty uncles and cousins, challenges and battles, stuffed my brain as if with old rags. As the tedium of his talk went on and on, I began to nod.

"Stay awake!" he cried, and stirred me with a slap.

"But what do these noble people have to do with me?"

"They are all about you!"

"*Me?* How?"

He glared at me, but as if provoked—and thereby probably skipping over several monarchs and their mossy mothers—began to talk about the current king, Henry the Seventh.

"His Christian name is Henry Tudor. Two years

ago, using five thousand Welsh and French soldiers, he treasonously killed the rightful English king, King Richard the Third, in a battle near a place called Bosworth. That noble king now lies in Leicester city at the Greyfriars friary in an unknown grave."

As I struggled to keep awake, the friar, eyes bright, spoke with increasing excitement.

"King Richard," he continued, "was a high and honorable lord. When Henry Tudor killed him, he dismissed Richard's court, placed the English crown on his own head, and his buttocks on the throne. Some thirty others of royal blood have far better claim to the throne than Henry has."

The friar had become angry.

"This Henry is a villain, a monster," the friar exclaimed, his voice growing ever louder. "He even murdered two young royal princes, Edward and Richard, both of whom would have been far better kings."

The murder of boys. *That* caught my attention. Was that about to happen to me?

"But," he rushed on, "there is yet *another* Edward, the Earl of Warwick, son of the late Duke of Clarence, Richard's brother, a boy who by every law, rule, and reason should be the true and right-ful king of England, since his descent is nearest to the crown. He's the one the people really wish to be their king."

"Why isn't he?" I asked.

"Henry Tudor imprisoned this Edward in the Tower of London. The boy, however, escaped. No one knows where he is, but *I* have found him."

It was then that the friar stood tall and cried out, "It is *you*, boy, who are the Earl of Warwick. It's *you* who are the rightful king of England."

TWELVE

NO SILENCE COULD have been more silent than that which followed his words. "Astounded" is too small a word to describe my reaction.

Except—I could not help myself—I laughed.

"You think . . . I am . . . *who?*" I mammered, sure my tiredness had puddled my ears.

"You . . . are the rightful king of England."

"*Me?*" I said, my eyes wide, almost as wide as my open-hanging mouth. "Me?" I repeated, hand over my staggered heart. "The *king* of . . . *England?*"

"And I," said the friar, "have found you."

I stared at the priest for a long moment and

almost laughed again. But then I understood: The friar was insane. Mad. Brainsick.

I searched for signs: crossed eyes, frothing mouth, a thick and hanging tongue. Though I saw none, what Brother Simonds said remained utterly daft.

"Brother," I said when I could finally find my voice, "I beg to tell you, what you've said is utterly wrong. I'm *not* who you say. I am *nothing*. I'm less than nothing. Ask Master Tackley. If that nothing could be cut in half, and all those halves cut into smaller bits, the smallest piece would still be . . . nothing. Nobody. Not royal in any way whatsoever."

"You are who I say," replied the friar, arms folded over his black-robed chest.

I studied him, equal parts puzzled and confounded. "Do you . . . do you . . . truly think so?"

By way of answer, he went down on one knee and bowed his tonsured head. "You are," he said, "my rightful king."

"Lambert the First?" I asked.

"Edward the Sixth."

There I was, a sorry, farthing-less, ignorant boy, for whom nobody cared, yet here was a holy priest at my feet insisting I was the king of England. Could anything be more fantastical? As I sat there, gazing at the top of his head, I giggled.

But when the brother remained on his knee, I began to grasp that he truly seemed to believe what he said. Did I believe him? Not for a moment! How could I? Me, England's king? It was preposterous. Beyond preposterous. Insane.

Nonetheless, the friar, still bowed, continued. "My duty is to help you gain your rightful throne."

I don't know how long I sat there and stared at him, trying to make sense of this madness. I could not. At last, weary of the jest, I yawned and said, "Please, Brother, since I am a king, may I have my first wish?"

"What is that?"

"I want to go to sleep."

"You will be up one floor. I'll sleep here."

I understood: He would be between me and the outside door—in case I tried to escape. Which is to say, I was in a cage, with a mad friar for a jailer.

THIRTEEN

BROTHER SIMONDS HANDED me one of the lit candles and had me go before him, up another flight of steps to a third level, which had a narrow hall. Never having been so high up before, I stood uneasily, pressing my toes on the floor to make sure the building was not about to fall. It seemed safer than the friar.

Off the hallway were two small rooms, empty except for some narrow rope-beds.

"Where shall I sleep?" I asked.

"Wherever you desire," said the friar. "Just don't attempt to flee. If anyone found you, you'd be punished as a traitor. Do you know what happens to traitors?"

"No, Brother."

"You would be hanged, but before you'd fully died, your guts would be stripped out through your stomach wall and burned before you, while your beating heart would be removed and stuffed into your bloody mouth. Finally, your body would be cut into four quarters and nailed about the town."

"God of mercy!" I cried, truly horrified. "Do you think me a traitor too?"

"I hope not. Now, say your prayers before you sleep. There's much work to do tomorrow."

"What work?"

"Making you king."

"But—"

"You'll do as you are told."

I found some comfort in hearing that old command: "Do as you're told." It showed that, despite the friar's lunatic words, I was still being treated as little more than nothing. I knew how to live with that.

Brother Simonds withdrew, but not before making a bow.

That time, since—as the saying went, only fools talked to fools—I just shrugged.

Yes, it was daft. But what was I to do?

FOURTEEN

THE FRIAR WENT down the steps, leaving me alone with but a feeble-flamed candle by my side. Darkness lay below. There were no sounds, save my flackering breath. Then a nearby church bell tolled midnight slowly. When it stopped, it left a deep, dead silence. At Tackley's there were always people about, always talking, always roistering. The soundless dark hollowed me.

Me, king!

I think I may have laughed again, or tried to, but it was false, empty laughter. I understood what I truly was: a prisoner.

I sat on the top step. The more I thought about the friar's words, the more outlandish my situation seemed. Beyond belief. As to *why* he had chosen to lay such a jest on *me*, I could not begin to guess. And what about that Earl of Lincoln? Did he also believe this absurdity? Me, who lived at the bottom of the world . . . going to the top.

Into my head came a picture of those players I had seen, in particular that player king with his fake crown, false beard, and wooden sword. Perhaps if I dressed like him I would please the friar. The thought made me smile.

But no, I reminded myself in haste, *I'm not a king, I'm a kitchen boy. A scullion.*

The candle faded out.

For a while I sat in the stone-still darkness. Then, on hands and knees, I scrabbled through the dark until I found a bed. Lying there I felt about my arms and my face, making sure I was still who I knew I was, Lambert Simnel, the dirty orphan boy, the muckworm.

Except the friar said I was royalty. The king of England.

I tried hard to recollect what I was *before* Tackley's.

In truth, I could not. As far as my memory served, my whole life had been at the tavern. No family. No friends. No memory of any other home. No remembrance at all, save that I was ignorant about everything.

It was as I lay there that I had a thought I'd never had before: Being ignorant meant I could not know what I was ignorant about.

From that, a new idea grew: Though I thought myself nothing—that did not necessarily make me so.

What if . . . what if . . . the friar spoke true?

"*You* are the rightful king of England," he had said, and bowed down, which no one had *ever* done to me before. Why would he do that if he didn't believe it? Surely he, a learned holy cleric, knew so much more than I.

I had always done what I was told because adults always told me what to do. Was not every adult a king to every child? Were not children *always* subjects to adults? I was no different. That meant that some adult, somewhere, at some time and place, must have told me to be a kitchen boy, and I *became* a kitchen boy—at Tackley's.

Now I was being told I must be a king. Did that mean I must become one? But what did I know about being a king? Nothing.

What, I wondered, was I to do if Brother Simonds persisted in this folly? If he did—and he owned me—and if others like the Earl of Lincoln, "the most powerful of English lords," agreed with him, what choice did I have but to do what I was told?

Into my thoughts came an image of Master Tackley bowing before me—the way the friar had done. That made me grin. *Me, the king of England. Tackley at my feet.* In truth, I liked *that* picture.

But it was silly. It would not, could not happen.

Deciding I must try to escape, I made my way down the stairs. Halfway along, I saw Brother Simonds on his knees at the bottom of the steps, blocking the way. He was praying. "Please, Lord," I heard him say, "forgive me."

I slipped back up the steps. Before I slept, I asked myself, *Do mad men ask forgiveness for their madness?*

My thoughts went back to that player king . . . and the piglet. How it had squealed . . . how people laughed. If I could be a player king like *that*, it might be sporting.

As I drifted off to sleep, the words "do as you're told" echoed in my head.

Did that mean I *must* be king?

FIFTEEN

IN THE MORNING I woke with three thoughts:

I am not the king of England.

Brother Simonds is a lunatic.

I must escape.

I looked around. When I saw some outside light coming in, I realized there was a window at the far end of the house. Hoping I might flee that way, I pulled the window open and looked out, only to see rooftops and a street *below* me. There were people too, moving about, as well as an ox pulling a wagon. Then a horse and rider went by. A bird flew by . . . *below*! I, who had spent my whole remembered life in a cellar, as if in a tomb—it made me dizzy to see such things from such a height.

I also noticed a soldier standing before the entrance of our house. He wore partial armor, and was helmeted, kettle style, with a sharp pike in hand. Was he there to keep *me* from running off?

Not able to cope with Brother Simonds's insanity, I wandered through the small rooms. They were not as empty as I first had thought. The people who had lived there must have left in haste, because things remained: a bit of cloth, a torn and pointed shoe, some bread. And, as I roamed, I noticed something under one of the beds. I pulled it out.

It was a round object, hardly bigger than my hand. Made of some dull metal, it was heavy for its size. One side was smooth. The other side bore an image of Jesus upon His cross.

My first thought was that it was some kind of token or pilgrim's badge. Only as I turned it over did I realize it was actually two pieces, held together by a tiny hinge. Some kind of casket. Curious about what might be inside, I pried it apart, opening it like a clam.

To my surprise a face peered back at me. I had found a mirror.

In my life I hadn't looked at myself very often. When I had, it had been in a puddle or gutter stream and therefore never very clear. Since this was a rare, clear image, I gazed at myself with interest. What I saw was a youthful, filthy face framed by tangled, tawny hair that reached my shoulders. A stub nose. Blue eyes along with a frowning mouth, round chin, and hollow cheeks.

I studied the face and asked myself: *Do I look like a king?* The only image I could conjure up was that player king, and I certainly did not look like him. Perhaps if I tied a beard on. . . .

I put the casket back where I found it.

Hungry, I went down the steps to the second floor, where I found the friar at his prayers.

I knelt beside him and listened, not that I understood his Latin words, but remained by his side until I heard a sound. A woman had come up the steps and into the room.

She was an elderly dame, with gray hair mostly

tucked beneath a cap. Her long dress was a deep red color, and she also wore a white apron. In her hands was a large basket.

Brother Simonds finished his prayers and looked about.

"Ah," he said to the woman, "you've come from the earl. What's your name?"

She curtsied. "Dame Joan, Brother. I've brought food and clothing."

"Excellent! Go muck the boy outside and take away his tatters."

Muck? I looked at the friar with puzzlement.

"Have you never been clean?" he asked.

"Why should I be?" I answered.

To the woman, he said, "Take him away!"

"Brother," I told him, "there's a soldier standing in front of the door."

"To protect you."

"From whom?"

"Your enemies."

"What enemies?"

"Many."

I shrugged. *There was no end to this friar's madness.*

To the woman, the priest said, "Get on with him.

The well is behind the house." He handed her a key and took a book from his pocket.

Dame Joan, after considering me with a pinched nose—as if to suggest that I smelled bad—made a motion with her hand. "Come along," she said.

Not wanting to go, I stood there until Brother Simonds barked, "Get on with it!"

I followed the woman down some back steps, out a door, and into a small yard surrounded by a high wall of brick. Far back was a privy pit and, in the middle of the place, a well.

It was the wall that interested me. I studied it to see if it was climbable. No sooner did I decide that it was and that I would than the dame said, "Strip off your clothing."

Upset, I looked at her with disbelief. Was I to stand naked before her?

"Hurry on!" she ordered, and dropped a rope-tied bucket into the well.

Reluctant, uncomfortable, I took off my tunic and stood there shivering, naked as a needle.

Next moment the woman drew up the bucket full of water and, without warning, flung it over me, the water so cold I yelped. Then, as if attacking me, she rubbed me all over with a rag. Not content with that, she doused me again, twice over.

Humiliated, my sole thought was to be at Tackley's where I understood what I was and how I would be treated.

The woman told me to return to Brother Simonds, so I reached for my tunic, my thoughts again on fleeing. But she kept my clothing from me. "Go back to the house," she said. "I brought better things."

The shame of running naked through Oxford kept me from escaping. Instead, I returned to where Brother Simonds waited. He put aside the little book he had been reading—the *Gospels*, I assumed—and handed me some clothes. To my surprise, they were the garb of wealth: dark blue hose; a rusty-red tunic with wide, puffy sleeves; a black leather belt, plus dark leather boots with pointed tips.

"What am I supposed to do with these?" I asked.

"Put them on."

"Truly?"

"Do as you're told!" he said.

I sighed and dressed myself in the new clothing but felt unnatural, as if bound by ropes. As for the boots the brother gave me—since I had never worn shoes—the stiff leather squeezed my toes. It was painful for me to stand, much less walk. I assumed it was a way to keep me from escaping.

Dame Joan reappeared and from her basket brought out scissors, for shearing sheep perhaps. I was commanded to stand still, while she clipped my hair until I felt my neck grow cool.

Her labor done, she was dismissed.

The friar made me stand before him while he studied me intently. Out of sorts, out of place, out of self, I stood there mute, feet hurting, not knowing what to do.

"Good," he said. "You are ready to begin your great labor."

"What labor?"

"Becoming king."

SIXTEEN

"YOU MAY START by eating."

At last—something sane. But when I moved to the table where food lay, I was mazed to see an egg and some meat, as well as white bread. Assuming only the bread was for me, I reached for it.

Brother Simonds cried, "Stop!"

I looked at him. *What now?*

"When you enter a room," he said with a glance at the book he held, "with other lords and ladies, you will say, 'Godspeed,' and with modesty, greet them all, holding up your head, while proceeding at an easy step from person to person."

I eyed him suspiciously. "Forgive me, Brother; there are no lords or ladies here."

"There will be."

"I don't understand."

"I'm telling you how a king must act. If you act like a king," he barked, "you will be king."

"With a false beard and wooden sword?"

Brother Simonds merely opened up his little book and began to read aloud: "'If anyone speaks to you when you enter a room, look straight at him with a steady eye. Listen well while he is speaking, showing a sweet face and good spirit. When you answer, be brief and to the point without chatter. Make sure you do not let your eyes wander.'"

"Forgive me, Brother, what book is that?"

"*Rules of Behavior.*"

"Rules? For whom?"

"Princes."

"Do princes have rules?"

"Of course," he said, and continued reading: "'Do not scratch yourself. Don't lean against a post, but always stand erect. Be always humble, carefree, and merry. Refrain from picking your nails, teeth, or nose. Cut your bread with a knife, not your hands.'

There's much more. You must learn it all."

"But what if I do itch?" I asked. "Surely I'll need to scratch myself. And why is it wrong to pick one's nose? At Tackley's Tavern people always do."

"You are a king!"

"Have kings no noses? No snot?" I countered. "Don't they itch?"

"You'll do as you're told!" he roared.

"I can do a jig," I said, doing a bit, thinking the friar would be amused by what I had seen the players do.

"Stop!" he said severely. "You must have dignity! Now eat."

Never mind dignity, I gobbled up the food.

During that entire first day, I did as the friar insisted, trying to learn his rules. As far as I was concerned, Brother Simonds was treating me like a dumb dog that must learn tricks. Except the things he said I must learn were all unnatural and seemed to serve no purpose other than to make me weary.

Once, I asked, "Don't kings have any joying?"

"They rule their kingdoms and tell their subjects what to do. They hunt, play music, dance, and eat."

"Are you my subject?"

"Yes."

"Can I tell you what to do?"

"You cannot rule others until you rule yourself."

"If I were to rule myself I would be a subject. But you said I was a king. How can I be a subject and a king at the same time?"

He frowned. "Humor does not befit your station."

Bad enough to be a prisoner. Far worse to be one when your jailer lacks all humor.

SEVENTEEN

BROTHER SIMONDS'S RULES took days and weeks to learn. Nor was it only rules I had to study.

To begin, my new clothing changed the way I walked, sat, and acted. In the past, I simply *was*. According to the friar, being a king meant I must do things as if I thought nothing about the world, while at the same time thinking about *everything*.

He said I must *talk* differently too. I needed to sound wise. How? Each word must be said distinctly, spoken slowly and without emotion.

"Like King Solomon?" I asked.

He took me seriously. "A fine example: Talk

with a show of indifference, though you know every word is important."

Day after day, as the lessons went on and on, the friar was so solemn and insistent that I began to think he truly believed that I *was* Edward, the Earl of Warwick, that it was I who had truly forgotten what I had been. Never, not for a moment, did he move from that.

He also insisted I must recall the names of England's great lords and ladies. Who was married to whom. Recall all "my" great uncles and aunts. Recall who "my" countless cousins were and speak of them as familiar kin. Though I remembered none of them, Brother Simonds insisted they *were* part of my households—I, who believed I'd never had *any* family. Or house.

He demanded I recall dates—I, who could not count beyond the ringing of church bells. He told me where I had lived. Under whose care. To whom I'd talked. Who had been kind to me? Who had not? When I protested that none of this was true, he assured me I had simply unremembered these things.

"You must sound well-witted," he said.

"You are asking me to be well-witted about stupid things." I threw back, my head hurting from his lessons.

He didn't care what I said.

One morning I hid beneath a bed. He dragged me out.

Another time I put on all of the clothing he had given me backward. He did not smile. He never did.

By way of practice, he constantly asked me questions about the person he said I was. What food I liked. What kind of games I played. My answers were almost always wrong.

"No!" the friar cried. "You must get it right."

Exhausted, I pleaded, "But why?"

"So you can be king!" he cried.

"It's too hard becoming king. I want to be what I was."

"What you were was Edward, the Earl of Warwick."

At night, I often asked myself: Why did Brother Simonds care so much about who and what I was?

When I finally learned the answer to that question, it changed everything.

EIGHTEEN

I DON'T KNOW how many days and weeks I remained in the house, seeing no else but Brother Simonds and Dame Joan. The world was gone from me, save the regular tolling of Oxford's church bells to measure time. Now and again, breaking the monotony, I heard passing bells, which counted out the years for someone who had just died. At times, I envied them.

I constantly tried to get Brother Simonds to laugh. He never would.

During the endless days of my learning, I was not allowed out of that house save to relieve myself at the skit pit. Even then, I was watched so carefully I could not escape. Each morning that soldier took up his position before our front door.

I admit, the food Dame Joan brought was fine. Meat. Eggs. Fair bread. Never had I eaten so well. She also made sure I washed my hands, face, and body and kept my hair trimmed. It being all unnatural, I hated it. Sometimes, when in my top floor space, I'd find dirt in a corner and rub it over me.

At night, alone, I used that mirror to study myself. As time passed, I began to change. I was becoming elegant and clean, a refined kind of person. I put on weight. My face filled. I rather thought I *was* becoming king-like. Quite often, I wondered what the Tackleys would think of me. Indeed, I never stopped thinking of running off, and constantly watched for a time when I might.

At last, that moment came.

One morning Brother Simonds informed me he would be gone for the day.

"Where to?" I asked.

"The Earl of Lincoln's court. He has asked me to report on your progress."

"What will you tell him?"

"That your memory has much amended. That you are becoming what you were and are meant to be."

There was something in his voice, an uneasy edge that made me ask, "Brother, are you afraid of Lincoln?"

My question made him frown. It took some moments before he said, "I serve him."

"As I serve you?"

Instead of replying, he gave stern instructions—and the house keys—to Dame Joan that she must make certain I kept to my lessons. He left.

When he was gone, I thought on the friar's words, that I was becoming what I was and am meant to be. It made me think on what I had been, and how I had changed. What fun it would be to show off to the Tackleys. Then I realized that with the friar gone, I had a chance to do just that.

I began by getting rid of Dame Joan. That wasn't hard. She had been instructed to wait upon me. Brother Simonds insisted I command her—as kings must, he said.

"Dame Joan, I want better meat than this," I told her, and shoved away the beef that lay on my trencher.

"Yes, my lord," she replied, which is what she had been instructed to say to me. She made her courtesies, said she would be gone for just moments, and left me alone.

No sooner did she go than I ran to the top story of our house and poked my head out of the window. I saw her walking down the street to the nearby butcher. I also observed the soldier, as ever, standing before the *front* door.

I rushed into the small backyard, with its surrounding wall of rough bricks, which made it easy to climb. Once over, I dropped on the far side into a rubbish lane. Dame Joan would never find me there.

At last I was free.

When I'd first come to the house where the friar and I stayed, it was during the night, so I was not sure where in Oxford I was. So I just ran, following the flow of people. Happily, they led me to the High Street, from where I easily found my way to Tackley's Tavern. Merely to see its steps filled me with gladsomeness and sent me all but tumbling down.

It was as always: fogged and fumy, tables crowded

with people at their cups and trenchers, the air filled
with gabbling voices, including Mistress Tackley,
loud and insulting all. In the far back, pig-bellied
Master Tackley stood among his pots and brew-
ing kettles. There even was another boy—quite
filthy—tending the fire and spit. It was as if I was
seeing my true life again. The hubbub never seemed
so soothing. I felt myself grinning.

But as I stood on the lower step, enjoying the
scene and people, a silence settled over all. Eyes
full of hostility turned on me, as if I were someone
foreign.

Next moment, Master Tackley lumbered forward. As he approached, he touched his forehead in
respect and, to my great amusement, made a little
bow.

"Yes, young gentleman," he said, "what might we
do for you?"

"Godspeed, Master Tackley," I replied, beaming
broadly. "Don't you know me?"

Tackley studied me with wary eyes. "Young sir,
begging your pardon but you're a stranger to me.
And forgive me, sir," he went on, "with all respect,
we don't have the refinements to serve such as you."

"But . . . Master, I'm Lambert Simnel!" I cried. "Your nobody spit boy."

Tackley's eyes widened, his cheeks puffed. "If it's Simnel you seek," he said, "I suggest you go to the friary. He was taken there, ages ago."

Utterly confounded, I stood stock still until I recalled that the clothing I had on was completely different from what I used to wear. I had gained weight. My face was clean. My hair was cut. It was as if I were in a costume. No wonder Master Tackley didn't know me. What's more, the unfriendly silence and hostile glares from the patrons made it obvious that I—in my new guise—was no longer welcome there.

More than anything, their eyes made me see that I had become someone else.

Frightened and confused, I retreated up the steps. But the moment I reached the street, I found myself surrounded by soldiers.

Nineteen

THERE WERE FIVE soldiers in all, dressed in the livery of the Earl of Lincoln's men. In their hands were poleaxes, by which they might pierce, pull down from a horse, or chop an enemy to pieces. At the moment, however, it was clear the only enemy was me.

"That's him!" I heard Brother Simonds cry.

The soldiers pressed in, while the friar, in their midst, grabbed hold of me. "To the house!" he shouted.

Whether I was walked or carried, I can't say. I only know I was taken through the town surrounded

AVI

and kept hidden by soldiers like some castle wall with legs. All the while, the friar pushed me, so I kept stumbling forward. "Hurry! Hurry!" he kept shouting.

When we reached the house, I was shoved inside. From within I heard Brother Simonds order the soldiers to be posted not only by the front, but at the back as well.

Thoroughly dejected, I crept up the steps to the solar, trying to think of something merry to say to soothe the friar. But he followed too quickly and stood over me. "You fool!" he shouted, and struck me hard across the face.

Taken by surprise, I fell to the ground, only to be dragged up and shoved down on a low stool. I had never seen him so frantic.

"Have you no understanding of what you are about?" he cried.

Twisted over with pain, shamed, I managed a snuffling nod, pawed my teary eyes, and tried to find some breath. "Forgive me, Brother," I faltered, "I just—"

"The fate of England rests upon you," he fairly spitted out. "Have no doubt, if Henry Tudor, the man who calls himself England's king, had you in his hands, you wouldn't live another day. Not half a day! That clumsed head of yours would be chopped off before you could take another breath."

Though I was crouched down, arms over my face, he roared on. "You *must* do what you're told! Or people will die."

"Die? Who will die?" I mumbled, hoping talk would lessen his anger.

"Many!" he shouted. "Including me!"

Truly baffled, I wiped away my tears, the better to see him. His tight-fisted hands were by his sides, so that his shoulders seemed narrower. His back was rigid.

"Why will *you* die?" I asked.

Breathing hard, struggling to control himself, he said, "What we are doing is . . . extremely dangerous."

"Why dangerous?"

"You idiot! There already is a king. There cannot be *two*."

"Please, Brother, I'm just—"

"Why won't you understand?" he cried, and for the first time I actually heard pleading in his voice. "Are you truly that stupid? You have one task. *One!*

You *must* be accepted as the Earl of Warwick. And you must begin by convincing Lincoln."

"But . . . what if that doesn't happen?"

"Then neither of us will live!"

"But please, Brother," I said, trying to keep him talking and me from weeping, "what if people *do* accept me as Warwick? What will happen?"

My question seemed to take him by surprise. "Then . . . ," he said, "then you will be king, and many others will—" He abruptly ceased to speak.

"Others will . . . *what?*"

"Become part of your court," he said. "And I'll find—God willing—a high place in the church."

My failure to fully grasp his meaning must have shown on my face.

"Like many," he said, "I was at King Richard's court. When Richard was lost, all was lost. My position. My wealth. I was cast out. Made *nothing*. And nothing is the way I began in life. Have you any idea how hard I worked to rise from nothing? If I am to rise again, I need . . ." He faltered, but I heard the anguish in his voice.

"Need *what?*" I asked, truly perplexed.

"*You!*" he cried in exasperation.

"*Me?*"

"Yes, you! Because when you become king you'll . . . you'll give us back what we lost."

I stared at him with disbelief. "Is that why you . . . why you've done this to me?" I managed to say. "So I would help . . . *you?*"

"Why else?" he cried in utter fury.

My thoughts were in turmoil. "Then it's . . . it's not me," I stammered, "who needs you. It's you . . . who needs *me*. To get what *you* want."

He opened his mouth as if to reply, but no words came. Only a quick nod, *Yes*.

"But . . . why did you choose me?" I whispered.

"Because . . . you . . . look like Warwick," he said.

"*Look?*" I howled. "What reason is that?"

"The English will only follow a true and close descendent of King Richard."

"And they will do so because I *look* like him?"

The friar's face turned sickly-white. It was as if in his rage he had misspoken and only now did he realize what he had said. With that realization his strength failed, he sank to his knees, closed his eyes, pressed his hands together in prayer, and silently moved his lips.

As I watched him, a whole new understanding

came: It was not love for me or England that had caused him to teach me all those princely things. He never thought me Edward. He was teaching me to be the Earl of Warwick so that he and others, maybe even Lincoln, could regain their positions. Why *me*? Merely because I *looked* like Warwick.

Neither of us moved. He was on his knees, praying. I was sitting there gawping at him, trying to absorb the full meaning of what he had done.

Shaken, I struggled to my feet. I'm not sure the friar even noticed.

Moving slowly, paying him no mind, I went down the steps to the front door and opened it. The soldier was standing on guard. He looked around at me.

"Brother Simonds wishes you to come to him," I said.

The soldier, unsure what to do, hesitated. I stepped back to let him pass me. He came forward and started up the steps. The moment he did, I leaped onto the street and began to run. Nor did I look back, or aim for anyplace, but dashed hab-nab though alleys and narrow byways until I came upon the Northgate and passed through the town walls.

Not only had I escaped Oxford, I had also freed myself from the friar.

TWENTY

I WAS BEYOND the town walls. Exhausted, I had to halt. When I saw the Church of Saint Mary Magdalen, I looked back to make sure I was not being pursued. As far as I could see, I wasn't. I sat down by the side of the church doors and tried to calm myself.

My head was bursting with what Brother Simonds had said: That he—and others—needed *me* to be the Earl of Warwick so he, and they, could regain their high positions.

There was no caring for *me* in that. It was merely how I appeared. When the friar told Lincoln I was "well-witted," that, most likely, was not true.

It was as Master Tackley said. I *was* nobody. I merely *looked* like some prince.

I tried to push down my swell of pain. Breathing was hard. Tears fell. To distract myself, I looked out upon the open space before the church. Many stalls, offering food or made goods, had been set out. People were coming and going, buying and selling. Some passed me on their way into the church. Not that they looked at me. I watched them, and wished I could be like them, going about my life in my ordinary way.

As I sat there, I became filled with anger at the friar for what he had done: the painful way he'd treated me; the arrogant and everlasting lessons; how insultingly he'd always talked to me; how, day after day, he'd made me work to be shaped so that he—I now understood—might regain what *he* had lost. The friar hadn't really thought me the Earl of Warwick. No. It was *nothing* about me. I merely *looked* . . .

I remembered his prayer the first night in the house: "Please, Lord," I'd heard him say, "forgive me."

I understood now what he was saying.

I assumed the friar would come after me, as he had done before. That meant I had to do something quickly, go somewhere. I only knew I couldn't go back to Tackley's. He had turned me away.

Not sure what to do, I continued to sit, looking out at the stalls. As I did, I noticed a very ordinary-looking man selling cabbages. There was something about him . . . a familiarity, though I could not think where I had seen him before.

Then I realized who he was: He had been one of the players. Indeed, he had been the first player king. Solomon. There he was without his beard, his robe, crown, or sword . . . selling cabbages!

I watched him intently, remembering how I had considered running away to join him and the other players. But they must have come from Oxford.

Into my head came what the friar had said to me: "If you act like a king, you will be king." Like the cabbage seller.

Being a real king—I supposed—meant I would be rich. Eat whenever I wanted. Have gaudy clothes. Tell people what to do. Play at games. Go hunting. Ride a horse. Good things, all. Things I had never done. And by doing so I would be *somebody*. Somebody grand. A king. People would bow down to me. Surely Tackley would.

I remembered something else. The friar had told me he'd begun as *nothing*. Look what *he* had become. If I let the friar teach me to be a king—that is to say, if I chose to be what *I* wanted—I might become something different. Well, yes, I could be a nobody. But also a seller of cabbages. Or a king.

Do what you're told. Could I not tell myself what to be?

I sat there going over this notion, knowing only that I liked it. A *kitchen boy or a king,* I told myself. If that man could sell cabbages and be a king, why should I not be what I wished? If Brother Simonds wanted me to be a king, a real king, I could be one.

The more I sat there, the more I thought I could.

The more I thought I could, the more I thought I would.

Being nobody, I had nothing—truly *nothing*—to lose. By playing a king, I might have everything.

At length, I got up, walked back through town, and returned to the house.

TWENTY-ONE

THE SOLDIER WAS not on guard.

I went inside and I climbed the steps to the second floor. The friar was on his knees, at prayer. He had a book in his hands. This time I was sure it was the *Gospels*.

He stopped his prayers and looked up at me. Hard to say what I saw most on his face: anger, sadness, embarrassment.

Neither of us spoke for a moment, until I said, "I won't run away again, Brother."

"It must *never* happen." He spoke hoarsely.

"No, Brother. Never."

"Have I your absolute word?" I could see enormous relief in his face.

"Yes."

He stood up and held out his book toward me. His hand was trembling. Never had his eyes been so intense. With his voice struggling to gain command, he said, "Swear!"

I put my hand on the book. Perhaps it was, after all, his book of rules. No matter. "I swear," I said.

It took him a moment before he said, "Very well. There is work to be done. Start with your lineage; let me hear you confirm who you truly are."

I held back my smile and said, "My father was the Duke of Clarence. His brother was Richard, Duke of York, late king and the son of Richard, Earl of Cambridge, who was the son of Roger Mortimer, the Earl of March, who was the son of Edmund Mortimer, Earl of March, who was the son of Lionel, Duke of Clarence, who was the son of Edward the Third, England's great warrior king. Therefore I am Edward, Earl of Warwick, the rightful but uncrowned king of England."

"Good!" cried the friar, vastly more at ease.

Did he believe?

Did he only want to believe?

Did I believe?

It did not matter.

The practice went on for the rest of the day. Other than the friar's unrelenting questions and my correct answers, the only different sounds were the church bells tolling the hours as they did every day. Yet, all had changed. I knew the role I must play.

When night came, I went to my bed, took up that mirror, and gazed at myself. I said, "Who am I?"

In the voice the friar had taught me to use, "I am the Earl of Warwick. England's future king."

I smiled.

My mirror image smiled.

In the many days that followed, Brother Simonds held me to hard learning and practice, but more kindly than before. That said, at times I grew so weary I cried, "Have I not learned enough?" and cry was what I did.

To which he would respond, "You must be perfect."

Do not misunderstand; I now truly wanted to play the part of Edward, Earl of Warwick. Thus I did all the friar told me to do, so after a while I could do so without any prompting, Warwick's words and actions flowed from me freely. Moreover, I was taught to count. I began to read. Any remembrance of my former life dropped away, like the dirt that had been washed from my body that first day.

Truth be told, I worked hard to think myself the earl.

I must have progressed, because one day Brother Simonds announced, "It's time for you to go before the Earl of Lincoln again. He needs to judge you and see what you are."

Observing tightness in his voice and body, I knew he was anxious about the outcome. It gave me pleasure to know that his fate was dependent on me.

So when he said, "Just remember: How he receives you will decide if you live," I smiled and returned, "And you, too, Brother."

"Aye," he admitted ruefully. "Me too."

TWENTY-TWO

THE DAY TO see Lincoln arrived. Morning was given over to practicing manners, walking, posture, words of greeting; quizzes about relations, where I had been, what I had done—all the things that the friar said I must know and be.

It made me very tense. In truth, I wished to pass this test.

Dame Joan brought new clothing from Lincoln, superior to what I had before: soft silks of many colors, new boots, and an embroidered jacket with threads of what looked like gold. I was given a cap, in which a fine feather had been placed.

"From what kind of bird did this feather come?" I asked, trying to be calm.

"A phoenix," the friar replied.

"I've never heard of it."

"You are one."

"What do you mean?"

"A dead phoenix rises from the ashes of what he was. Like you."

"And you, too," I reminded him, but he was not amused.

Before I put on the new clothing, Dame Joan hauled me outside. As a soldier stood by, I was washed and scrubbed until my body fairly rippled with her rubs. My hair was cut, shaped, and scented.

At dusk, just before we were to leave, I stole up to my room and looked at my clean face in the mirror. "I am the Earl of Warwick," I said. "The rightful king."

At the time of departure, Brother Simonds informed me that he would throw a cloak over me and have our two soldiers carry me to the Earl of Lincoln's home.

"Can't I walk?"

"There can be no dirt on your feet."

"Like a saint," I said, trying to make light of it.

As usual, he did not smile.

I asked, "Will I see Lincoln alone, like the last time?"

"Francis Lovell will be there."

"Who is he?"

"You know of him as Viscount Francis Lovell."

Taking the hint, I recited what I'd been taught: "Lovell was one of the most loyal supporters of our late good king Richard. His Lord Chamberlain. A rich and mightiful man, Lovell helped Richard rule the kingdom and fought with him at Bosworth. He is among England's greatest soldiers."

To which the friar added, "But never forget that if King Richard had died a natural death, he made it clear he wished Lincoln, his nephew, to become king."

"He did?" I said, taken by surprise.

When the friar said nothing, I said, "Brother, if Lincoln had been promised the crown, is he truly willing to let *me* be king?"

Brother Simonds put a hand on my shoulder. His piercing eyes had never seemed sharper. "Do not," he said, "ask that."

Taken aback by his severity I said, "Why?"

His answer was to throw a cloth over me. Next moment I felt myself picked up. I knew that I was being carried along and sensed when we left the house.

As we went, I kept thinking about Brother Simonds's refusal to answer my question about Lincoln: *Is he truly willing to let me be king?* Why hadn't the friar answered? It was as if I had come upon a sack that seemed to be full. But when I looked within—nothing was there. Yet, the very emptiness seemed heavy. It was a riddle to me.

A short time later I was set down, the cloak whisked away. I looked about. Brother Simonds and I were just inside the entryway of the hall where I had first come to stand before the Earl of Lincoln.

The doors were locked behind us. The great wheel that hung from the ceiling bore no burning candles. There was no fire in the hearth. It was darkful.

At the opposite end of the room, two men were standing in front of that long table. The shorter one was Lincoln. The other, I supposed, was Viscount Lovell. He appeared powerful, and his strong gaze was solely on me. His eyes were clear and fine, his mouth set tight.

As I stood there, working hard to contain all my feelings—excitement, worry, fear—the friar pushed me forward.

I moved toward the two men, trying to walk the way I'd been taught, with dignity and purpose, looking at them with steady eyes. I could only hope they did not hear my pounding heart.

I halted a few feet before them, made sure I was standing straight, and in my smoothest voice said, "Godspeed, my lords."

Viscount Lovell stared at me. "Who are you?" he asked.

"My lord, I am Edward, Earl of Warwick. My father was the Duke of Clarence." I went on to give my whole lineage back to King Edward, concluding by saying, "My father's nearest kin was Richard the Third, the true king of England."

When I was done, the two lords exchanged looks. I thought Lovell allowed himself a smile.

Lincoln, his eyes as hard as before, his mouth set in a severe frown, drew close and studied me. It took all my strength not to shrivel.

He began to ask me questions, questions about where I had lived, who had taken charge of me, what people I had seen at this court, that court. Lovell asked more questions. It didn't matter. Brother Simonds had instructed me so well I was able to give complete and calm replies to everything.

The more I spoke, the more at ease I felt, answering without hesitation. So when Lovell said, "My lord, how were you able to escape from the Tower?" I barely paused before saying, "I had friends whose names had best not be spoken."

There was a moment of silence. Next moment Lovell let forth a shout of satisfaction. "The perfect answer!"

Turning to the priest, Lincoln called out, "He shall do!"

When Lincoln and Lovell retreated into a corner and talked in low voices, I remained where I had been, trying to stay calm. From time to time they glanced at me, but I could hear nothing of their words. I kept still, forcing myself not to look at the friar. All I wanted to know was, had I convinced them I was Warwick?

Lincoln lifted a hand and wiggled his fingers. "Brother Simonds," he called. The friar went over and the three spoke, their voices low.

Lincoln picked up a purse from the table and handed it to Brother Simonds, saying, "It's time to go forward."

"I think," the earl continued, loud enough for me to hear, "the boy should be seen. Let the word go out: Young Warwick is free and ready to claim his rightful crown."

"And on to Ireland," said Lovell. "Where we have powerful friends."

Nothing was said to me, the player king.

TWENTY-THREE

BROTHER SIMONDS and I walked out of the hall. The moment we were beyond hearing, I stopped, tugged on his cape, looked up, and said, "Lincoln believes I'm the Earl of Warwick, doesn't he?"

"He does."

"Then shall I live?"

"You shall," he said, and for once actually smiled.

The jolt of joy that went through me was such that I abruptly hugged the friar, which made him laugh (the first time *that* had happened) as he hugged me back.

Catching my breath, I said, "Brother, I need you

to say it again: Am I truly going to be king?"

"Do you think you will?"

"I do!" I cried

"Then you will be," the friar proclaimed.

"I am Edward!" I shouted. "Edward, Earl of Warwick!" Then I poked his stomach. "I shall make *you* a bishop."

He grinned and laughed again.

Never had I felt so happy, so full of joy. And what came into my head? I wanted to rush off to Tackley's and make him bow down before me.

Did I? Of course not. Tackley was beneath me.

The friar and I returned to the house in a different fashion than when we'd left. I went on my own two feet, with no cloak to hide me. Two of the earl's servants went before us, carrying flaming torches to light our way. Behind me marched some soldiers, pikestaffs in hands. Brother Simonds was by my side, a smile on his face, hands clasped before him, as if in grateful prayer. No doubt his prayers were being answered.

As for me, I was light-headed, cock-brained, hardly knowing whether to laugh or cry. I wanted to jump about and shout, "I am Edward, the Earl of Warwick, and I am going to be king!"

We paraded grandly down the middle of the street, so that people had to make way for us. Many stopped and gazed at me. Ragged children ran alongside, trying to see who I was.

"Hold your head up," Brother Simonds urged. "Acknowledge with grace the people who are looking at you."

"How?"

"Lift your hand and wave."

When I did, people bowed, removed hats and caps, and touched their foreheads in respect.

Never had I such fun.

We reached the house. "I'm pleased with you," said the friar.

"You must use words of greater respect," I returned, putting on a grave voice. "You need to say, 'My lord, you did well.'"

My words took the smile from the friar's face. For an instant, I feared he was going to strike me. The next moment, however, he said, "You are quite right . . . my lord." And bowed.

We both laughed, but my laughter, I think, was truer. There was a moment when we looked at each other. I held my eyes steady. *He* looked down. I think it was only then that he realized he had made me his master.

As if to restrain me, he said, "We'll continue your lessons, but starting tomorrow you'll walk through town at least once a day."

"Why?"

"You heard Lincoln. You must be seen so people will know you as the true claimant to the throne."

"Brother, he knows who I am, but I don't think he likes me."

The friar's look turned dark. "You'd best keep that to yourself."

"Why?"

"He's your protector."

"Should I be afraid of him?"

"Lincoln is my lord, but it's you who are going to be king."

"I want to be," I said, sparking with the night's success.

"But you're still a boy."

"What does that mean?"

"You'll need advice."

"From you, of course," I said, mockingly.

He would not smile. "The Earl of Lincoln is my lord."

"And I told you," I said, raising my voice, "I don't like him."

The friar put a hand on my shoulder, making me look up at him. "My lord, here's as important a lesson as I can give you: The man who is close enough to help you up is near enough to push you down. Now go to sleep."

In my room, I reminded myself it had been my finest day. Yet, now that I was alone, I was edged by unease. I knew why Brother Simonds wished me to succeed. But the Earl of Lincoln hardly needed a place in court. What did *he* want of me? It had to be something beyond my looks.

TWENTY-FOUR

EACH DAY DURING the next week, I returned to Lincoln's great hall. I went openly, dressed in different clothing—all costly—supplied by Lincoln. At my side, Brother Simonds. Armed soldiers, in the earl's colors, walked before and behind. "Make way for the Earl of Warwick!" they called.

What sport it was to see people on the streets stop and show their respect for me by doffing caps and bowing. I even heard someone shout, "Long live the Earl of Warwick!" People truly believed I was Warwick. I waved my hand to thank them like a lofty lord.

Let me make one thing certain: From this time on, as far as I was concerned, I *was* the Earl of Warwick. All I did, thought, and said was shaped by being him. Never again would I be called a *nobody*. I was heir to the throne of England. I was Edward, the royal prince!

At Lincoln's court, there was music—trumpets, lutes, rebecs, and sackbuts such as I had never heard before. I mingled with powerful people, adults, elegant lords and ladies, people whose names I didn't know. They bowed to me, fawned on me, brought me dainty food and drink, asked me questions, most of which, thanks to Brother Simonds's teaching, I answered with ease. When I couldn't answer, he, always by my side, might say something like, "My lord, I think you must have forgotten . . ." and provided an answer. I'd remember those responses, so when asked again, I had his words like arrows in my quiver, and if required, I could send them home.

How delightful it was to have so many mighty people treat me with such respect. How pleasing to be the center of everyone's attention. To have my every request fulfilled. I was loved by everyone. Or almost.

At these gatherings, I would be in the middle of a flattering crowd, enjoying the attention of all. Then I'd notice Lovell and Lincoln at the edges of the room, standing apart, Lincoln watching me closely with his large, dark eyes, stroking his ruddy beard, as if amused.

They never talked to me. Never engaged with me. Enough, or so it seemed, simply to have me there. It was as if my person brought them to the edge of something that I didn't know about and was not to be told.

Then I learned some of those things.

Brother Simonds and I were coming home from the earl's court. It being night, torchbearers were with us, as were soldiers.

"Will I keep doing this?" I asked the friar.

"Next week we go to Ireland."

"Where is that?"

"Across the Irish Sea."

"A sea!" That stirred me. "How will we get there?"

"By ship. We need to reach the city of Dublin, where your father—the Duke of Clarence—was born. You'll find many friends."

"What am I to do there?"

He smiled down at me. "You'll be crowned king of England."

"Truly?" I cried, greatly excited. "With a real crown?"

"It shall happen."

As we walked on, I kept asking the friar how my crowning would be done. When? What ceremony? What place? Though he wasn't sure about details, he was happy to join in my elation.

But then that other worry came back. "Brother, do . . . do Lincoln and Lovell truly want *me* to be crowned?"

"They want justice to be done," he said, which I thought somewhat slippery.

"What will happen to them when I become king?"

He didn't answer.

Trying to tease out an answer, I said, "They're always watching me. We never speak. They seem to be waiting. For what?"

"To make you king."

"Brother, when I am king will I be able to tell them to go away?"

The friar glowered. "Why would you do that?"

"I told you. I don't like them."

The friar abruptly stopped, reached out, and as he used to do, gripped my shoulders tightly. Speaking in a low but urgent voice, he said, "I've warned you, never say that."

His fierceness startled me. "Why?"

"Without them you are *nobody*," he whispered. "It's *they* who will determine your future."

His change of manner, his alarm, his words, made me look up at him. "Brother, are you the Earl of Lincoln's friend or mine?"

He turned away and stared into the air as if trying to find an answer. When he did speak, all he said was, "No more empty talk." He started to walk fast, as if to leave my question—which he had never answered—behind.

We went on in silence until a new thought came. "Brother," I said, "that false king, the one called Henry, what about *him*? Am I allowed to say he's my enemy?"

"Absolutely. You must."

"Will he honor me?"

The friar snorted. "He'd much rather kill you."

"*Kill me?*" I cried, coming to another halt. The thought had never occurred to me. "But why?"

"I've told you. There can't be two kings. If you are the Earl of Warwick, the true king, Henry Tudor cannot be England's king. Besides, as king, you will decree who the traitors are."

"Would he truly . . . kill me?"

The friar nodded.

A shudder swept through me. "But . . . but then . . . what am I to do about him?"

"You need to kill him first."

I stood there, astounded. "How could I ever do that?"

"You'll send your army to fight him."

My head was whirling "*Army? What army?*"

"The army the earl is gathering for you in Ireland."

"He is?"

"An army of thousands."

"What are . . . thousands?"

"As many people as live in Oxford."

I looked at him with disbelief.

"That's what it will take."

"You are teasing me," I said. "None of this is true."

"More than true," he answered. "Necessary. What's more, you're going to lead that army back to England, to oppose Henry."

"I am?" I said, increasingly mazed. "*Lead* an army?"

"It must be done. Before Henry kills you."

Thoroughly alarmed by such talk, I just stood there, studying the friar's face to see if he was in earnest. He seemed to be.

It was great sport to be the Earl of Warwick . . . but killing . . . being killed. That frightened me.

"Brother," I said, "didn't you once tell me that King Richard had decided that, if he died, the Earl of Lincoln, his nephew, should become king?"

"I may have."

"But . . . King Richard *did* die."

"Henry took the crown."

"But when I use my army to kill Henry, I, not Lincoln, will be king. Is that right?"

Once again, the friar did not reply. All he said was, "We need to go home."

I held him by his sleeve. "Brother, you never told me that being the Earl of Warwick meant a lot of killing."

He said nothing, but walked on.

I came along, but now I was terrified. It was as if I were back in the time when Brother Simonds took me from Tackleys. No, not the same thing: greater fright. I would have to kill or be killed.

Alone in my room, I tried to make sense of all the things the friar told me were about to happen: going to Ireland, wherever that was. Being crowned king. I liked that. Leading an army, an army of thousands—whatever "thousands" meant—against King Henry. Surely, if Henry knew I had such a vast army, he would run away. Then I wouldn't have to kill him. I prayed that would happen.

But what if Henry did not run away? What if he tried to kill me first?

I don't think I had ever truly thought about what being killed *meant*. I tried, but I couldn't. All I could do was shudder.

What if I couldn't lead an army?

Would Lincoln really let me become king? Was he my friend or enemy? What did he really want from me?

What if people learned that Brother Simonds

had taught me to be what I'd become? Would Lincoln still let me be king?

Too many questions!

I decided there was only one answer to everything: Be like a king more than ever before.

TWENTY-FIVE

A FEW DAYS later, the Earl of Lincoln, Viscount Lovell, Brother Simonds, and I left Oxford, setting forth for Ireland, where I was to be crowned. Once crowned I would gather my army, invade England, and kill King Henry.

I, Lambert Simnel.

No.

I, Edward, Earl of Warwick.

I kept thinking on the friar's words: *If you act like a king, you will be king.*

Yes, I would be a king.

When we left Oxford, it was late harvest time.

Tree leaves were brown, the air clear and sharp. Here and there, fingers of white frost etched the rutted road.

A troop of mounted soldiers accompanied us, some in front, and others behind, some to either side. The steady clink of harness and the rolling rumble of horses' hooves on the hard mud road measured the time. The soldiers wore iron battle hats, called barbuts, which covered heads and ears, so only narrow faces showed. Over their chests were brigadines, jackets of linked metal plates with chain-mail sleeves. Having these men so close did much to ease my fright about King Henry trying to kill me.

They made me feel more king-like than ever.

Lincoln and Lovell, also mounted, were in bright and burnished partial armor, swords on their hips. By Lincoln's flank, a soldier held up his battle pennant: the cross of Saint George with three rampant lions, in gold, blue, red, and white, stirring to behold.

In our train were several ox-pulled wagons, carrying the necessaries for our journey: food, clothing, armor, and tents. The oxen, however, obliged us to move at their slow pace.

I rode behind Lovell and Lincoln, Brother Simonds by my side. To my great joy, I was on a fine horse, a gift from Lovell. Having never ridden before, it took some learning and soreness, but I was told I sat bravely.

I wore a green padded tunic, red hose, and leather boots. High gloves, too. A round, soft hat made of Flanders felt. I had my own small sword on my hip. It made me feel powerful to have it.

Was there ever—I kept telling myself—a boy on such a glorious adventure? *I am Edward, Earl of Warwick. These are my soldiers. I am powerful. I am the king to be.* I repeated these things to myself over and over again. I wanted to believe them. I *did* believe them.

Even so, Brother Simonds's cautions nipped at me, making me feel I wasn't full master of my fortune. I blamed him for my worries, my doubts.

I turned to him, "How much longer will it be before we get to Dublin?"

"We need to reach Minehead village first. A hundred miles away. On the sea. Ships will be waiting there to take us to Dublin."

"Will that take long?"

"The weather will decide."

"You'll come to Dublin with me to see me crowned, won't you?"

"I pray so."

"Aren't you sure?"

"It depends on the earl's wishes."

"Not mine?" I asked, resenting his timidity toward Lincoln. When he didn't reply, I said, "Brother, I thought I was your king."

"You are, my lord. But as I've told you many times, it's the Earl of Lincoln who protects us both."

His words irked me. Was I not his lord? Lincoln was below me. The friar needed to act in response to *my* wishes, not the Earl of Lincoln's. I felt I needed to find a way to make the friar acknowledge this. That led to another thought that increasingly worried me: What if Brother Simonds told people how I was when he found me? They might doubt that I was Edward. Treat me with disrespect. I wanted Tackley's bellowed words—*You're a nobody! Nobody!*—completely out of my head.

I was thinking about this when we passed some peasants with scythes in hand cutting the last stubble corn in the fields. As we went by, they stopped working, doffed their caps, and bowed. In return, I lifted a hand to acknowledge their respect.

As it happened, one of the peasants did not bow. Seeing this, Lincoln called out a command and a soldier went and struck the man so that he tumbled to the ground.

At first I felt sympathy for the peasant. Then I realized he had shown me disrespect and deserved his drubbing. Was I not the future king? Reverence was owed.

The incident reminded me of my wish to show Brother Simonds that I was his lord. I told myself, *I must act like a king.*

I saw my way. Urging my horse forward, I drew up beside Lincoln. Brother Simonds, as I knew he would, moved with me, staying close.

I called to him loud enough so the earl would hear. "Brother, how did you come to know so much about me?"

"I spent time at King Richard's court, my lord. I saw you, the young Earl of Warwick, quite often."

Though I knew this was not true, I held back my smile. Instead, I asked, "Brother, were we friends at that time?"

"Of course."

"What happened?"

"Henry put you in the Tower," said the friar. "And you were clever enough to disappear. Happily, I found you."

"Do you remember what I was like when you found me in Oxford?"

The friar was scowling, clearly puzzled as to where my questions were tending—which, let it be said, amused me.

"Do you?" I pressed, enjoying my joke.

"I do, my lord." He offered a false smile.

"Brother," I went on, "you must never tell anyone what I was at that place. It was beneath my dignity. I don't wish it ever to be known."

As I had hoped, Lincoln heard the exchange. He looked around, curious to catch the friar's reaction.

I pushed on. "Brother, do you recall that time I ran away?"

"I do."

"You struck me. Do you remember *that?*"

Lincoln looked back sharply. The friar was no longer smiling. "For your own good, my lord," he said softly, his face red with embarrassment.

I said, "You struck me just like we hit that peasant who would not bow to me."

Brother Simonds looked at me with unease. Sensing his weakness and my strength, I went on with my mocking. "Am I not your master?" I asked.

"You are," he said glumly.

"Brother, I command you never to tell people how you found me. Or how you hit me. I don't want people to think less of me."

"May you grow to be ever more yourself, my lord," said the friar. He let his horse slow down so as to fall back.

Enjoying the friar's discomfort, I laughed and turned to Lincoln.

"Lincoln," I said, "do you think Brother Simonds knows too much about me?"

"What do you mean, my lord?"

"Didn't you just hear his answer about his time with me in Oxford? He was being disrespectful, was he not?"

Lincoln kept silent a moment, glanced at Lovell—who had not uttered a word—and said to me, "I shall speak to him."

I let my horse drop back, the clip-clop of the

horses' hooves echoing my thoughts: *I can tell people what they can and cannot do. I am England's most powerful person. Ha! King Lambert the First!*

It was hard to keep from laughing aloud. But that laughter would have been short-lived.

TWENTY-SIX

I FIRST SAW the village of Minehead from some high bluffs: a cluster of stone buildings under thatched roofs, a church with a square tower, and an inn. Most importantly, it lay close to the sea.

Never having seen the sea before, I was entranced. The blue-gray waters seemed to go on forever. Closer in, great waves rolled over brown sand. A stone path stuck out from the sand into the sea. Some small boats were tied to it. The air bore a salty smell while overhead, large gray birds circled, squawking incessantly. I told myself they were welcoming me.

Offshore were two large floating *things*. Not sure what they were, I was reminded of floating pin-pillows. These were high in back and front, with one big pole in a scooped middle section, and other sharp poles poking from all angles.

Brother Simonds pointed to them. "Those are the ships," he said, "which will take you to Ireland and your coronation."

"Ships!" I cried with delight. "Can they cross the sea?"

"They will."

"You don't seem happy," I teased him.

"You complained to Lincoln about me."

"You said *he* was your lord, Brother, not me. You helped me recall I was the Earl of Warwick. Have I not learned well?" I laughed at the friar, amused to see him feel rebuked.

Pressing his thin lips together, he said nothing, only bowed his head. Not wishing to ride with him, I cantered forward to be with Lincoln.

As we entered the village, people came to greet us. Though they were low, poor folk, Lincoln had me go to meet them, a herald going first, calling, "Here is Edward! The Earl of Warwick. Your true king!"

When people acknowledged me, I was generous in my greetings. My attention, however, was all for those ships. How were they made? How did they move? Not wanting to show my ignorance, I didn't ask.

Some of the soldiers who came with us were billeted in town houses, but most were placed in small tents set up on the common. I, along with Lincoln and Lovell—and their close servants— were put into rooms in the village inn.

My room was a tiny garret space with a low, slanted ceiling. There was a narrow feather bed, and one small window at the gable end. Once led there, I was told to remain until called.

With nothing better to do, I thought to look out the window, which was plugged by a piece of wood with a grip. Grasping it with two hands, I pulled it free and leaned out, hoping to look at the sea, and the ships. The window, however, faced the other way. All I could see were the bluffs and the road, which our company had just traveled.

As I peered out, I saw a solitary horseman moving slowly along that road, going away from the village. Astride his horse, he was stooped as if burdened. It took a few moments for me to realize it was Brother Simonds.

He was leaving! I immediately felt a deep and painful stab of regret, realizing it was probably I who had brought about his going when I told Lincoln he had ill-treated me. As I watched him move over the highlands and disappear, I wanted to shout out that I had only been teasing. That he should come back. That I had not meant it truly. And with those thoughts I grasped to what a degree he was my most important friend, my teacher, the one upon whom I most depended upon for advice. What would I do without him?

I thought of appealing to Lincoln, only to understand that if I did, it would make me appear weak. Better to act as if the friar's banishment was *my* doing, *my* power.

Indeed, the friar's words once again came into my head: *If you act like a king, you will be king.*

That was when I realized that if I were to achieve this fully, I must put the Earl of Lincoln in his place.

I sat quietly, thinking out what I must say and do.

TWENTY-SEVEN

EVENING. IN THE dining area, a fire was burning in the hearth. Smoke leaked into the room, which made the air close. Lovell and Lincoln were seated at the inn's warped table, upon which food was heaped: roasted birds on their trenchers and bread, along with cheese, chunks of turnip, and jugs of drink. Small, half-withered apples lay about.

The two lords were stuffing their mouths, grease dribbling down their chins and beards. Listening to their boisterous talk and the way they slurred their words told me they had already drunk too much.

When I sat down, nothing was said to me.

I remained there, staring at the hearth and its fluttering flames, trying to find my resolve, knowing I had to put Lincoln in his place—beneath me. Now and again a spark sprang from the fire, landed on the brick floor, and faded.

Do not fade, I told myself.

"My lords," I began, drawing myself up, "I'm glad you paid heed to me and sent Brother Simonds away. You should know that, as your king, I will not let anyone treat me poorly."

Lovell barely paused in his eating. Lincoln, with indifference, said, "You were right. We've no more use for him."

"Besides, the friar wasn't cheap," added Lovell.

"But I assure you, my lord," Lincoln said to me, "we amply rewarded him." The way he said "my lord" was soaked with scorn.

"And did you not get a fair return?" I said.

Lovell and Lincoln exchanged a look. Then Lincoln took a deep drink, cleared his throat, turned to me, and said, "Surely you know I paid the friar to choose a boy who looked right and then teach him to become the Earl of Warwick. And"—he flapped a slack hand toward me—"he did."

It took a moment for me to fully understand his words. They filled me with anger.

"The friar didn't *choose* me," I returned hotly. "He *knew* me at King Richard's court. When I escaped from Henry's Tower prison, he searched me out. Found me. I *am* Edward!" I shouted.

No one spoke. The only noise was the crackling of wood in the fire. As if snickering. After a moment, Lincoln shoved food into his mouth and belched. It was Lovell who, after swallowing more ale, reached out to pat my hand with his greasy fingers. "Excellent. It's always better when the storyteller believes his tale."

I stood up. "But, my lords, it's a tale that you, too, must believe."

Lincoln and Lovell exchanged glances. I was sure I had made them uneasy.

Lincoln looked up at me. "Lambert Simnel. Isn't that what you told me your name was? So I would think, *boy*, you might be happy enough to have people *treat* you as *if* you were the Earl of Warwick. Enjoy it while you may and know it serves *us* well. I suggest you sit down and eat. It won't be there forever." He went back to his food.

I remained standing and cried, "I *am* Edward. And I *shall* be king."

"You certainly look and act like Edward," said Lincoln, trying to make a jest of my words.

"My lords, I challenge you: Do you have a better choice than me?"

That stung them into silence. Lincoln tapped the table with one agitated hand.

"My lords," I said, "let it be understood. I *am* the rightful king."

Lincoln glanced at Lovell and then said, "Once Henry Tudor is defeated and killed, the Earl of Warwick is the next in line."

"That's me!" I cried, then sat back in my chair, gripped the arms, and glowered at them.

A flush of anger filled Lincoln's face. He turned to me: "Be advised, boy, what can be found, can be lost."

I could have no doubt: He was threatening me. It set my whole body to trembling. I flung myself forward and said, "My lords, you should know that after I'm crowned king, I intend to pick the people I want to have near me."

No one spoke until Lovell said, "We sincerely hope you choose us."

"Because," said Lincoln, "you don't want to become a traitor to yourself. Do you know, *boy*, what happens to traitors?"

"Brother Simonds," I said, "taught me that as king, *I* will decide who the traitors are."

They stared at me, alarm filling their faces. I felt as if I had won.

When they made no reply, I stepped from the table and went to my room. Once there I sat alone, much pleased with myself. I was sure I had over-awed them.

If you act like a king, I reminded myself, *you will be king.*

Perhaps it was then that I realized it would not be enough that I chase Henry Tudor away. I must arrest Lincoln, and have him beheaded.

TWENTY-EIGHT

IMPATIENT TO BE in Ireland and crowned, I fretted about the friar, worried about Lincoln, and paced about my small room a great deal. I was told we had to wait for the right wind to take us across the sea. Every moment we didn't sail weighed upon me like a sack of stones. I kept to my room, preferring to be alone. Now and again, I was called below to meet people. Lincoln, with a false display of deference, would announce, "Here is your king, Edward the Sixth."

Citizens, often of high quality, but many low, would bow down before me, kneel, and say things like, "Long life, my king." Or, "God give you much grace, my lord." Or even, "You are my true king." They gazed upon me with respect. Some kissed my hand.

I replied with a kingly display of smiles and aloofness as befit my station. After giving thanks for their love, I returned to my room, where I endlessly contemplated how I might strike at Lincoln.

At table, though I sat with Lovell and Lincoln, I barely listened to their talk. With no appetite, I leaned back in my chair, arms folded over my chest, eyes half closed. I loathed them.

They pretended to have no interest in me. But I could see—to my pleasure—that while they had made me apprehensive, they too were uneasy. I kept wishing the friar would come back, but I knew that would not happen.

Indeed, something else happened.

It was our third day at Minehead, and we were at table when a messenger galloped in, bringing a dispatch for Lincoln. He read it, passed it to Lovell, and then turned to me. "News about you has reached London."

I looked up. "What news?"

"You are worrying King Henry. He fears you."

"I'm glad," I said, with a surge of hope. "Has he fled?"

Lincoln gestured to the message in Lovell's hands. "He has found a boy who looks like you: a fair-headed, blue-eyed boy, much your age and height. Calls him Edward. He's parading that boy, proclaiming to the world that that boy is the true Earl of Warwick.

"In other words," Lincoln went on, "Henry is saying that you, my lord, are an impostor." As he spoke, the earl kept his eyes on me. His face was all a question, as if wondering what would be my response.

"But . . . that's a lie," I said. "I'm the Earl of Warwick."

Lincoln laughed. "Good! I'm glad you know it."

To which Lovell added, "But you are certainly upsetting Henry."

"But who . . . who is that boy?" I demanded, taken aback by the notion of another Edward.

"That London boy?" said Lincoln airily. "Some"— he smiled—"scullion, perhaps."

Much stunned by such a notion, I tried to react

steadily, only to stammer, "But . . . but to say that you are someone other than you truly are is . . . is sinful."

"It's only what we would expect from such a liar as Henry Tudor," said Lincoln.

Lovell leaned toward me. "Therefore, my lord," he said, "we are pleased that you show yourself for what you are, the true heir to the throne. The true Earl of Warwick. The world must see you bold and strong." His words were soaked in sarcasm.

"I *am* Warwick," I said with as much force as I could muster.

"Of course," said Lincoln, his voice full of mockery.

I sat there, desperately trying to make sense of this London Edward.

The two of them, Lovell and Lincoln, held still, smiling and gazing at me, as if expecting me to say more.

Under their mocking eyes, the best I could think to say was, "I promise you, my lords, I shall be all that I truly am."

"Excellent!" cried the earl. "Do so and you will serve England—and yourself—best."

I wanted to leave the table, but did not wish to show them how upset I was.

Lincoln picked up the message and appeared to reread it. At length he folded it, then tossed it on the table.

To Lovell he said, "What do you make of it all?" He spoke as if I were not there.

"I assume the message is true," said Lovell. "We've made Henry anxious enough so that he has taken Edward from the Tower and is parading him about. Does that concern you?"

"Not a bit," said Lincoln. "I know Edward well. He may be the real prince, but he's a brittle boy. I assure you"—he gestured toward me—"we have a far better Edward here."

The words pierced me.

Lincoln made a mock bow in my direction. "Brother Simonds chose well: You really do *look* like a prince. And thanks to him, you act like one. People will much prefer to believe in you. That Edward—he may be the prince, but he plays the part so badly." He leaned toward me as if revealing a secret. "The truth is, he's simpleminded."

I jumped up and shouted, "I am the real Edward!"

"Well played!" cried Lovell. He clapped his hands.

"I am!"

Lincoln said, "It's as you said: We have no choice."

They laughed.

I tore back to my room. Once there I sat dazed and horrified. In London. Another Edward.

I tried convincing myself that the London boy was *not* the real Edward, but merely someone Henry had made. Or that the message that came to Lincoln was a fraud, meant to confuse me and throw me from my rightful place. Was *that* what Lincoln meant when he had said, *What can be found, can be lost?*

Increasingly panicky, I considered running off. Then Lincoln would have no Warwick. He'd regret then how he treated me. Meanwhile, I'd make my way back to Oxford. But . . . it was miles away and I had no idea how to get there. Besides, what would I do if I reached Oxford? I didn't want a life at Tackley's. I wanted to be what I'd become: Edward, the Earl of Warwick.

I wanted to be king.

Brother Simonds and Lincoln had gathered me up and worked me so as to turn me into Edward. The friar had betrayed me, used me, so he might gain a position at court. Lincoln was doing the same for his own reasons, reasons I still didn't know.

Never mind. There was only one thing I could do. I told Lincoln he had no choice. I realized then that I had no choice either. I had to make the lie come true. It did not matter who I was. To save myself, I *must* become the king of England.

TWENTY-NINE

THE NEXT DAY I was informed the weather had much improved. We had the winds to cross the Irish Sea.

All was astir. First, Lincoln's and Lovell's belongings were taken into small boats and brought to the ships. Horses were carried out and hoisted aboard with slings. Our soldiers were marched down and rowed out.

When all was ready, Lincoln, Lovell, and I boarded a small boat. As we pushed away, some of the Minehead people—including a priest—stood and blessed us as we went off. "Long live the Earl of Warwick," they cried. "God save King Edward the Sixth!"

I lifted my cap and called out, "God give you grace!"

"Brother Simonds taught you well," murmured Lincoln into my ear.

I did not look at him.

Once on board, a man whom I was told was the ship's captain did us reverence, to me in particular. Then I stood upon the high, rear part of the ship and watched as sailors sprang around the masts like imps. Brown sails were loosed, hoisted, and filled with wind, as if quickening with life. Within moments, the ships heaved about, gently rose and fell, rocked from side to side, and began to move out upon the open waters of the sea.

I looked back. It seemed as if England were sliding away, growing smaller until it became no more than a dusky strip on the lowering eastern sky. I recalled what Brother Simonds told me: that when I returned to England, I would be leading an army. I tried to imagine how grand it would be, me upon a fine horse, in bright armor, sword in hand, leading my soldiers toward a fast-retreating Henry.

I could not help wondering where the friar was.

When I was king, would he come to my court? Never mind how he treated me. I'd give him a high position.

When I faced the other direction, the Irish Sea opened without boundaries. Though the wind was cold and full of salt spray, I spent most of the day staring at the ocean, trying to imagine the moment I'd be crowned.

Before the day was done, I saw a band of green land. "Ireland," I was told.

Our ships sailed into a wide area, land on both sides. Before us was the entry to a wide river. Since it was growing dark, our sails were furled, anchors dropped. Lovell was taken by a small boat to the city. With Lincoln beside me, I stood by the ship's rail, and as night thickened I looked upon Dublin city and its scattered lights.

"The lights," I said, "remind me of a smoldering fire."

"Do they?"

"Waiting for a blow of breath to spring into a blaze."

"As you shall set all England on fire," said the earl.

I didn't tell him I was thinking of Tackley's,

of my life turning mutton over the fire. If Master Tackley could see me now, what would he think?

Having become suspicious of everything, I asked, "Where has Lovell gone?"

"To arrange your welcome, my lord. Tomorrow will be an important day. You must show yourself with full majesty, so you'll be accepted and treated with dignity. It needs to be done well. You should know there are still some people here who will require convincing."

"Convincing of what?"

He smiled. "That you are Edward. Act with grandeur and you'll be crowned."

"I am Edward," I assured him, and meant it—but not for him. For myself.

That night I slept in a tiny room somewhere within the ship. Outside my door, Lincoln had placed a soldier—there, I suppose, to keep me. It said something of Lincoln's worries that he felt the need to hold me caged.

Did Lincoln hate me as much I hated him? Then again, he and I knew who I truly was. We were joined by what we could not speak. Our lie made a bitter bond.

THIRTY

NEXT MORNING OUR ships came back to life as we sailed up the river so I could view Dublin for the first time. Never before had I seen so large a city. It was set upon a hill, sloping down to the wide river. At the hill's summit, like a crown, stood a great church. The city proper was walled round with dark gray stone. Within the walls were many thatched-roof houses crowded together. More houses were outside. Along the river's edge, just beyond the city's wall, was a wooden quay, where ships tied up to unload.

At the northeast corner of the city wall, over-looking the river, was a round tower, no doubt to keep watch. Three huge monastery buildings were pointed out to me, and a vast castle loomed. I was told it was the largest in Ireland.

"That's your castle, my lord," said Lincoln. Then he pointed to the great church on the summit. "And that's Christ Church Cathedral, where you'll be crowned."

All I could think was, *Almost king.*

Our horses were unloaded first. Our soldiers went next, after which they mounted and formed a double line. Finally, Lincoln and I disembarked, me in my finest clothing.

Lovell was waiting for us.

On shore, we got on our horses, had Lincoln's standard hoisted, and made a stately progress between the soldiers, entering Dublin by way of a great stone gate.

Beyond the gate, we were met and welcomed by crowds of clerics, lords, and citizens, brilliant in multicolored robes and dress. The Archbishop of Dublin was pointed out to me, as was the Archbishop of Armagh. More importantly, I saw (as I was told) the greatest lord in the country, the Earl of Kildare. He saluted me in grand fashion. I returned as much.

Welcoming speeches were made to me. Gifts were given. I listened to the speeches as if every word had grave import. As for the gifts, I was generous in my thanks but never touched them, since they were whisked away by Lincoln's servants. He kept them.

Most importantly, I could see and feel that these Irish welcomed *me* as their true king. Crowds of people of all kinds and quality lined the streets, acknowledging me with adoring cheers. "Long live King Edward the Sixth! God save our king."

Here I was already a king.

We reached Dublin Castle. It was a massive fortification built of the same dark gray stone I had seen everywhere. High towers guarded each of its four corners, and a small river, like a moat, ran to the south and east of it. Did not every boy want his own castle? I had one.

With the blaring of horns and the beating of drums, we entered the castle from the northern side, going through the first gates, a barbican that was flanked by two more tall towers. As we passed under it, I could see the portcullis gates—like sharp teeth—ready to bite.

Beyond the stout outer fortification, we moved

along a tunnel, which cut though a massive curtain wall, into a wide and open bailey. There, hundreds of Irish soldiers were waiting to greet me.

When I rode in, these Irish troops rushed forward—momentarily alarming me—only to stop short and cry out a roaring welcome. "*Ard Rí na hÉireann!*" they shouted, which, as I would learn, meant they'd greeted me as the high king of Ireland.

Astride my horse I turned to Lincoln and said, "Lincoln, this is *my* army."

He nodded but said nothing. I wondered what he was thinking.

Off to the right was a great hall, the King's Hall, or the donjon, as they called it. First, however, we went to a small church, St. Mary del Dam, within the castle walls. Before a statue of Our Lady, a priest gave thanks for our safe arrival in Ireland. As I knelt, I gazed upon the serene face of Mary—who was wearing a beautiful golden crown—and prayed fervently that she would be by my side in times to come.

Next, I was led into a hall, wide and tall, with huge beams above. Many tables had been laid out, all spread with heaps of food.

The feast was endless; the speeches, all addressed to me, long. I sat in a great chair, which I fancied was a throne. Oh, how I worked to listen, pretending sincere interest in the words. Then I had to greet many important people who approached with much bowing, kneeling as they proclaimed their loyalty, their belief in me, Edward, Earl of Warwick.

During the long welcome, some tumblers came in to turn and twirl in fantastical ways. The performers made me remember those players in Oxford. I recalled the platform on which that interlude was played. What a greater stage I had! Even so, I wished that false king could see me now. I could teach *him* how to play a true king.

Meanwhile I watched as Lincoln and Lovell went off in a corner and conferred with various lords and clerics. I had no doubt they were plotting for their own future. We three were moving along the same road. I wondered if they had any suspicion that I intended to go a different way and leave them behind.

At length, to my great relief, Lincoln and some local lords led me to a large room where there was a fine bed and oak furniture. I was told this was to be my room while I was in Dublin.

The others who had attended me bowed away so only Lincoln and I remained.

"You did well," he said.

"What happens next?" I asked.

"We need to assemble a larger army. Bigger than the one Henry used to overthrow Richard. Once that's done, you'll lead your army back to England and defeat Henry Tudor."

I nodded, hoping my trembling would not be noticed.

"I promise you," said Lincoln, "that false king Henry is hated by all. As soon as we land in England and news of your arrival spreads, people will flock to you. Your army will be vast." He gave his untrue smile and turned toward the door.

Maybe it was because we were alone. Perhaps it was his smile, in which I had had no faith, or that I had seen him conferring with others, but I suddenly called out, "My lord, do you see how the people flock to *me*, not you."

Lincoln paused, turned, and considered me. "Of

course. As you are the rightful heir, my lord, it's only natural that they turn to you."

I said, "Brother Simonds told me King Richard chose you to succeed him."

"Alas, Richard only *said* it. By the laws of succession *you* are meant to be the king. It's you the people will follow, not me."

"Is *that* why you needed me?" I cried out. "Because an army would follow *me*—the Earl of Warwick— but not you?"

He stood very still. I had not the slightest doubt that I had guessed right and that we now knew each other perfectly. He the high one. I the low. He the adult. Me the boy. But he had made me greater than himself. He'd turned me into what he needed. Now I was more powerful than him.

"My lord," was all he said, "you will be meeting many people. I suspect some will ask you how you managed to escape from the Tower of London. Best not to mention Brother Simonds."

"What shall I say?"

"You need to show them how brave you were."

"I know nothing about the Tower."

"Tomorrow, Lovell and I will tell you all you

need to know. Good night." That time he did not bow. The door closed. I heard the lock clack shut.

When Lincoln left me, I lay on the soft bed and thought about the great army I would be leading into battle. I had no doubt Lincoln was right. As soon as King Henry knew we were coming, he would flee in fright.

Or so I hoped.

Then I would deal with Lincoln.

Would he flee too?

Or would he turn on me?

THIRTY-ONE

I WAS TAKEN to Dublin's Christ Church Cathedral—along with Lincoln—by his Grace, Walter Fitzsimons, the Archbishop of Dublin, a small old man of deep but soft voice, which he used slowly.

"Here, my lord," the archbishop said to me, "is where you will be crowned."

I looked about in wonder. I had never seen such a great building. There was an immense nave of five bays of triple arches on each side, each bay surrounded by vast pillars. Its elaborate walls were light in color, in contrast to the multicolored glass windows, colors I could not begin to name. Carvings everywhere. In front of the choir stalls I could see the sanctuary, and beyond that the Lady Chapel. Nothing that had happened before made my becoming king as real as that moment. The wonder of it!

"You shall march down the nave," the archbishop informed me, "with Lords Lincoln and Neville by your side. The lords of Ireland will follow. I'll proclaim you and crown you Edward the Sixth."

At that point, the archbishop paused, and turning to Lincoln, I asked, "Have you a crown?"

Lincoln hesitated, as if puzzled, before saying, "I shall get one."

Later that day, we returned to the castle. As soon as we entered, Lincoln said, "The crown."

When he headed for the small castle church, I followed. He strode in and approached the statue of Our Lady. To my great shock, he reached up and plucked the crown from Her head. "Now we have something for your coronation."

In stealing Mary's crown, I was sure he had committed a grave sin. I was sure something bad would follow.

I was right.

The next day, Lincoln asked me to meet with the Archbishop of Armagh.

"I am tired of meeting people," I said. "Do I have to?"

"Anyone who can lend you support is important," Lincoln told me. "Moreover, he insists upon meeting you alone."

"Why?"

"I have no idea. Now, do as you're told."

I knew what those words meant.

I sat in a large, leather-padded chair in a small room when the archbishop came. He was an old, stout man, dressed in flowing robes, which bunched upon the floor so that he seemed to be in a state of melting. Moreover, he came forward with small, halting steps. His old hands, much wrinkled, were, I noticed, shaking.

He drew close, paused, and peered up at me from under shaggy eyebrows. His eyes were watery. I waited for him to speak, but he continued to stare at me, until, in a raspy voice, he said, "Boy, who are you?"

Startled, I said, "I am Edward, Earl of Warwick," and repeated my lineage.

When I was done, the archbishop just stood there and continued to look at me.

Then he said, "Boy, you are *not* who you say you are. I knew the young Earl of Warwick at King Richard's court. You look *something* like him—the same color hair and eyes. Somewhat his size. But you are an imposter. A nothing."

The archbishop's words jolted me. I wanted to speak, to deny what he said, but he lifted a shaking hand to silence me.

"The Earl of Lincoln has tried to convince the world that you are the true Earl of Warwick. You, poor, misled boy, have gone along with him. You are his tool to attract an army. The people won't follow Lincoln. They will follow a Warwick. You can pass as him. But once you're in London, Lincoln will have no more use for you. You'll stand between him and the throne."

His words brought back all my alarms and fears. I had no idea what I could say.

"Beware, boy," he went on. "To take the throne, Lincoln must kill you. And he will. May God have mercy on your soul." The archbishop made the sign of the cross, bowed, turned, and slowly left the room.

I sat there truly quaking. It was hard to breathe. To swallow. I felt terribly alone in that room. There could be little doubt, two people wished to kill me: Henry and Lincoln.

I formed a plan: The moment I heard word of Henry's surrender, I would have Lincoln and Lovell arrested and executed. I told myself that they could have no idea what I was planning. I convinced myself that *I* was in control.

THIRTY-TWO

MAY 24, 1487. A most splendid day!

In the great nave of Dublin's Christ Church Cathedral, during a magnificent ceremony, I was crowned King Edward the Sixth of England. During that ceremony, long and solemn, I worked hard to appear grave. But in my head I called myself *King Lambert the First*.

Among the thousands in attendance (in and out of the cathedral) were the bishops of Cloyne, Meath, and Kildare. And many great Irish lords, among them Sir Roland FitzEustace, and the Earl of Kildare. Lincoln and Lovell were witnesses, of course, along with the commanders of my army. So too were minstrels, heralds, singers, and musicians.

I was draped in robes of crimson and white, along with green silk slippers. Walter Fitzsimons, the Archbishop of Dublin, placed the crown on my head, proclaiming, "God save Edward the Sixth!"

The people roared, "God save Edward the Sixth!" When that happened, was I solemn? Not at all! I was grinning, overflowing with delight. I was England's king! I had done it. It may seem absurd, but what came into my head? I wished Master Tackley was there.

I confess my favorite moment came when I was hoisted upon the shoulders of Lord Darcy of Platen, said to be the tallest man in Ireland. He carried me out and about the streets of Dublin, where throngs cheered for me. How they loved me! To all, I threw groats newly stamped with my sovereign name, Edward the Sixth.

After much banqueting in the castle, long speeches, and much homage and music, I stole out at night and slipped into that small church, St. Mary del Dam. There, I replaced the crown that had been stolen from Mary's head. I also fell on my

knees and asked forgiveness. I also gave my thanks
to my Lady that I, Lambert Simnel, a want-wit, a
muckworm, a nobody, a boy with no more worth
than a spot of dry spit, had become king of England.

If ever there had been a miracle, I was one.

Even so, I knew I needed more miracles to make
sure I held my kingship.

THIRTY-THREE

ONCE I HAD been crowned, a parliament was convened, which proclaimed my rule in England and in Ireland. I tried to make sense of the things that were said, the speeches made. I did understand that some Irish traitors were denounced, their lands seized. The rest I found boring. Once, I admit, sitting there, I fell asleep. I had to be nudged awake, only to find the eyes of the assembly all on me.

My days in Dublin passed much too slowly, though they were filled with many gatherings during which I had to meet the great men of Ireland. The most important were Gerald Fitzgerald—Earl of Kildare—and his brother Thomas Kildare. Also Sir Roland FitzEustace, a great Irish lord. They treated me and spoke to me as their lord, their king. Just as Lincoln predicted, they asked me how I had freed myself from the Tower of London.

Happily, Lovell and Lincoln had tutored me and described the Tower in great detail. I told a story that was bold, full of dangers and miraculous escapes. The more I related it, the better it became, as I learned to hold my audience's rapt attention. All the same, I was careful not to reveal the names of those who'd helped free me, saying I must protect them from the wrath of King Henry.

Each day I walked through the streets of Dublin distributing groats, the ones that bore my name. Citizens crowded to see me, showing their devotion and respect for their king. How they cheered when I passed.

In the many weeks that followed, a larger and larger army was assembled. The most important of those to join me was Martin Schwartz, who came from across another sea, from Europe. A famous Swiss soldier, he was renowned for his fierceness. Short and stocky, thick with muscles, his swaggering air forced one to look at him. He made a speech to me, with many a bow. His language being German, I understood none of it, but I was told that he and his soldiers vowed to support my right to the English throne, though it might mean their deaths. I gave a speech of thanks in return. I don't think he knew what I said. I had this thought: *We are all players*.

Lincoln informed me that having these Germans absolutely assured me victory over Henry.

These German soldiers had great mustaches and wild hair. Each carried two swords, one attached to his waist, another, much longer, in hand. Their helmets were round and fit closely over the head, like a skullcap, while body armor covered their chests and legs down to their knees.

My Irish soldiers had no armor, were generally bearded, had bare feet, and carried broadswords and long, sharp daggers, what they called *scians*. Their strength and a certain wildness made me love them.

Some English soldiers also came to us. Lincoln informed me we had gathered an army of eight thousand. That was far more than Henry used to defeat Richard at Bosworth.

Meanwhile, Lovell was working hard to secure ships to carry these troops to England.

I had no doubt that Henry was quaking.

During this long time, Lovell also gave me instructions on how to use a sword. He being one of the great knights in my kingdom, his instruction was the best. I was on my way to becoming a fine soldier, he said.

Finally, on a bright clear day, my army, with me in the first ship, sailed down Dublin's river. The cheers from those on shore were delightful to hear. I was their young warrior king. Thus we set out upon the Irish Sea with God's good winds speeding us toward England's shores.

I had no doubt: I was invincible. And I was on my way to London.

THIRTY-FOUR

HAVING GOOD WINDS, it took just hours to reach the Furness Peninsula along the English Cumbrian shore. By the time we got there, the day had turned blustery, with weighty clouds scudding overhead. The area chosen was bleak, desolate, and muddy, with little vegetation on the rocky shore. The only life I saw were circling sea birds, whose constant squawking suggested they took offense at our arrival.

By agreement, I was the first to step ashore, and with Lincoln and Lovell just behind me, I went down on my knees. Having practiced my words, I proclaimed my right to the crown of England loudly, denounced Henry as a usurper, and prayed: "Judge me, O Lord, and favor my cause." It was the same prayer, I had been told, that Henry had made before defeating King Richard. Oh, how well did I know my part!

The soldiers began to disembark.

We were met and welcomed by Sir Thomas Broughton—a knight who had been loyal to King Richard and who had fought with him at Bosworth. He brought a few troops to add to our force. These soldiers were the first of what I was told would greatly swell our numbers. My hope grew that Henry, hearing of my landing and of how many soldiers I had, would flee.

The bay we had entered was deep, so our ships, which had to go back and forth to Ireland to bring every soldier, had no problems. Nonetheless, it took two days to gather our entire army on land. The enormous force—more than eight thousand men— fairly bristled with swords, spears, mareskipes, bows, guns, and halberds.

I took to wandering among the troops, watching them work and hone their weapons, sharpening, fixing, or practicing with them. How they loved it when I, their young king, mingled among their ranks.

I told them they were unbeatable and said how splendidly they would be rewarded when we defeated Henry in the battle soon to come. These words always brought cheers; the cheers, in turn, gave me extra strength.

On June the fifth, we gathered our forces together and began heading east. Lovell, Lincoln, and I were in the vanguard, leading what was meant to be a quick march deep into England. I was mounted on a black horse, dressed lavishly, with a burnished breastplate that had been made just for me, my own sword at my side. A soldier with my new-made standard rode nearby.

Was this not what every boy wished for, to lead a glorious army to victory? I felt great excitement, and told myself I was full of courage.

Somewhere south, I knew, was the tyrant Henry, with whatever pathetic forces he had raised. I kept reminding myself that my soldiers would defeat him roundly and then I'd go on to be crowned again in London.

We passed Newby Bridge, Castle Bolton, and

Middleton. When we reached Jervaulx Abbey, we turned south in the general direction of the city of York. Over five days, we traveled more than two hundred miles, a great rate. As Lovell explained, the faster we moved, the fewer troops Henry could muster. It was Lovell's desire to maintain a constant offense.

Every night we—Lovell, Lincoln, that Swiss soldier Schwartz, and I—met to review our progress.

One night Schwartz and Lincoln got into a furious argument.

It was explained to me that Schwartz had been told by Lincoln that as we passed through England many more English soldiers would join our army because I, Warwick, now the crowned king, was leading the way. These new troops, increasing our strength, would make the defeat of Henry that much easier. I had heard Lincoln say so myself many times.

Those new men, however, had *not* appeared.

Lincoln insisted that they would still come.

Schwartz called Lincoln a fool, and warned him that unless we gained in strength we could be defeated. Lincoln accused him of being cowardly, which made Schwartz storm away to be with his own German soldiers.

Lincoln and Lovell were left sitting in dismal silence. All of this alarmed me greatly. It was clear things were not going well. I tried to make sense of it.

"Is Schwartz right?" I asked Lincoln. "Do we need more men?"

"Of course not," said Lincoln, and he, too, walked off.

Lovell and I remained alone. He must have seen the worry on my face.

"My lord," he said, "when Henry defeated Richard, he had only five thousand soldiers."

"How many did Richard have?"

"Six thousand."

"How could he have lost?" I asked.

"Treachery."

I said, "Lincoln told me we have eight thousand soldiers. How many does King Henry have?"

"We don't know."

"Truly?" I cried.

Lovell left me. Sitting there, alone, I was very frightened—nay, terrified. I tried to imagine what would happen to me if King Henry defeated us.

I remembered what Brother Simonds had said: *If Henry Tudor had you in his hands, you wouldn't live another day. Not half a day! That clumsed head of yours would be chopped off before you could take another breath.*

Though I sat near the fire, I felt icy cold. *Will I live?* I asked myself. I felt a sudden need to pray. Then I had a new realization. Brother Simonds had taught me many things, but he had not taught me how to save my soul.

THIRTY-FIVE

CONTINUING OUR MARCH south toward Henry, my army moved deeper into Yorkshire. On the night of June the tenth, we had news that greatly cheered our soldiers, and me. That night, at Bramham Moor, outside Tadcaster, Lovell led two thousand men on a night attack against supporters of Henry, led by someone named Lord Clifford. The result was an overwhelming victory for my side.

Then, just outside of Doncaster, Lincoln encountered some of Henry's forward cavalry under the command of Edward Woodville, Lord Scales. For three days, they clashed in and about Sherwood

Forest, the fighting forcing Lord Scales back to the city of Nottingham.

While successful, the fighting slowed our forces down. Our scouts were now telling us that King Henry and his army were advancing steadily. We also learned that during this period of time more and more soldiers were gathering to *his* side.

None joined us.

By June the fifteenth, we had reached a large open space southwest of the ancient village of Stoke. It was high and had a fine view of the lower country near the River Trent. Lincoln and Lovell surveyed the land and decided that it would be best if we took a stand on that ridge. It appeared we had little choice. I heard the talk and understood. Henry was fast approaching with his troops, as were his principal allies: the Earl of Oxford, plus the Lords Shrewsbury and Strange. He was bringing in other troops.

We gained none.

I was feeling more and more panicky. I dared not say it, or show it. I must play the king.

That evening we had a council with our commanders. Though I did not speak, I was there.

Agreement was soon reached as to how our forces would be deployed along a three-quarter mile ridge—the high ground—extending from Burham Hill to Willow Rundle. It was further agreed that we would begin by attacking Henry's troops at the hour of nine.

"How many soldiers," I asked, "does King Henry have?"

No one spoke for a moment, until finally Lincoln said, "From what we have been able to learn, we think he has some fifteen thousand."

"Fifteen thousand!" I cried, my stomach tumbling. "But—"

Lovell cut me off by saying, "The Lord's will shall be done."

That number, *fifteen thousand*, kept repeating itself in my head. Another number also echoed: the number of troops *we* had. *Eight thousand*.

How I wished I had never learned to understand numbers.

When the meeting was over and only Lovell, Lincoln, and I remained, Lincoln said to me, "You must ride among the soldiers. They need to know you are still with them."

Though too numb to say anything, I followed them to where our horses were tethered. We mounted.

"Lincoln," I found tongue to ask, "when the battle begins, where am I to be?"

"You will be behind the lines," said Lovell, "with a small troop of cavalry. You must be seen to be in safety."

I felt some relief.

But then Lincoln added, "If you are killed, or captured, it could cause panic among our troops."

How I wished I could be somewhere else. But all I said was, "Am I to do anything?"

He grimaced. "Stay alive."

The three of us moved among our soldiers. Some were grouped about small fires. Others lay asleep. Some played cards or rolled dice. When we passed by, they came to their feet and gave out cheers. "Warwick! Warwick!" they shouted.

Now and again I managed to say a few words to encourage them, but in truth, these words were merely in my mouth, not my heart.

I was posted behind our army, along with five English soldiers who were to protect me.

That night, as I lay upon the ground, I heard the

neighing of horses, the stamping of hooves. The constant clink of harness. The constant whispering of prayers. Now and again I heard the sound of plucking bowstrings, the music of war. I stared up at the night sky, wondering where I would be the next time the stars looked down at me.

Who am I? I kept asking myself. *You are Edward the Sixth, King of England. Invincible.*

But I did not sleep well.

THIRTY-SIX

JUNE THE SIXTEENTH, 1487, dawned another fair day. The smell of sweat, horse dung, and burning wood filled the air. That air felt heavy, ready to burst, as if just before a thunderstorm. I heard the beating of drums along with the blaring of trumpets. The trumpets sounded like souls crying for mercy.

From the ridge where I had been placed, I could see the River Trent to the west, rolling hills to the east, and flat lands to the south. Our army was already deployed and appeared in a state of agitation, as if all the men were shivering with emotion. The sharp, spiky points of staff weapons, pole-axes, pikes, bills, and halberds fairly bristled, and seemed to vibrate.

The Swiss and German troops, under the command of Schwartz, were in front. They were our best soldiers.

Behind them were the Irish. They still had no armor or shields. Rather, they carried long daggers and javelins. Mingling among them were contingents of our English troops.

I saw Lovell's standard and his soldiers to the right. Lincoln's men were to the left. In the early eastern sun, the burnished armor flashed like fire flares.

Only when I looked to the south did I see King Henry's army for the first time. The sight gave pain to my soul. His numbers seemed huge, much larger than ours. Horrific to behold and no more than a mile away.

Now trumpets continually blared from our side only to be answered from the army across the way, challenge and answer, answer and challenge. Like increasingly frantic hearts, drums beat faster and faster. Horses whinnied. Men shouted slurs and insults. "Warwick! Warwick" I heard. From afar came, "Henry! Henry!"

The battle was about to begin.

Near nine o'clock, I saw movement among our men. They had formed themselves into something vaguely wedge-shaped, a massive arrowhead, aimed right at the heart of Henry's lines.

Now, in orderly fashion, they began to press forward, slowly at first, then trotting, finally running. The speedy march of their feet sounded like the rattling of many dice in a wooden bowl. I felt the very earth atremble.

Across the way King Henry's army also began to move. Slowly and methodically, they tramped toward us so that I was minded of the steady rolling waves of the sea on that Minehead beach.

Now the air was filled with random shouts and cries that might just as well have been the bleating of cattle or sheep.

Now the two armies came to one another, hurtling forward with greater and greater speed, as if drawn together by some awful force.

Now Schwartz's crossbow men stepped out of line and loosed their bolts, only to quickly retreat into the mass of our forces so as to rewind.

I saw some of Henry's men fall. How quickly death came.

From where I stood, I saw Henry's troops suddenly divide. Bowmen stepped forward, in numbers I could not begin to count. In terrible unison they lifted their bows and bent them back, the arrows aimed high. Next moment came a sound like the plucking of a mighty string—the harp of God.

Now came a great hissing sound as the air filled with thousands of steel-tipped arrows, so that the air seemed streaked with lines, a sky of lines, as each bowman loosed arrow after arrow, ten a minute. The arrows rose in a high arch only to plunge down among our troops.

Some shields raised. Even as they were raised, many men fell, pierced mortally by arrows.

Now the air was full of screams and cries of pain.

Simultaneously, our advancing forces struck King Henry's lines, sounding a sickening *thud*. The force of this attack made their soldiers roll back. I winced even as I felt a surge of joy. But just as fast, Henry's forces held, reformed, and pushed back, and once again began to advance toward us steadily, their standards snapping in the air like barking dogs.

Now the advancing armies became so intermingled it was impossible for me know who was who, or who was on which side. Rather, the mass of men had become a writhing, seething knot.

Swords flashed. Battle-axes rose and fell. Flags whipped in the air. Trumpets kept sounding along with the beating of drums. The soldiers hacked, thrust, and stabbed at one another. Horses reared, plunged, screamed, and fell. "King Henry! King Henry!" came the cries, only to be answered by, "Warwick! Warwick!"

Now I saw the ground fleam with blood.

Now Lincoln's standard fell.

Now my army began to retreat. Faster and faster did they flee. All around me soldiers ran like rats before cats.

Now my army had been routed. Henry's army pursued, chasing and hacking down my soldiers by the hundreds. Arms broken, severed. Guts tumbled. Heads rolled down to the bottoms of deep gullies, where they lay forever still.

Now—in an astonishingly short time—the battle was over, our soldiers in desperate flight.

We had been defeated.

THIRTY-SEVEN

HORRIFIED AND BEWILDERED, I was so shocked I could hardly breathe, think, or move.

I am not even sure when the five soldiers who had been posted to guard me had fled. It took me moments to realize I was alone on my trembling horse. He snorted. He shook his head. The bridle jangled. He flicked his tail.

Not knowing where to go, what to do, I remained where I was, truly petrified.

Before I could move, a man in armor appeared, walking slowly toward me, sword in hand, slightly raised. *Was he going to kill me?*

My own hand shaking, I raised my sword. It seemed very heavy.

The man lifted his helmet and showed his face. "I am Sir Robert Bellingham," he announced. "In the name of King Henry, I arrest you, Lambert Simnel, for high treason."

For my part I managed to stammer, "I . . . I am Edward, the Earl of Warwick. Why do you call me by that other name?"

"Brother Richard Simonds has—in return for the king's mercy—told us all about you, including your real name. You are only Lambert Simnel."

I let my sword drop to the ground.

I would learn, later, that the Earl of Lincoln was killed in the fighting. Martin Schwartz also died, as did four thousand of our troops. As for Viscount Lovell, he may have been killed, or escaped, no one knew for sure. He was gone, never to be found.

As for me, Sir Bellingham grasped the reins of my horse and led me silently away, moving carefully among the dead and the dying. The air filled with moans, screams, and cries. I saw dead soldiers stripped of what they had. I saw the wounded being killed. I saw the death of thousands.

"Where are we going?" I finally asked, wanting only to go somewhere, anywhere, but where I was.

"You are to be taken to King Henry."

Into my head came Brother Simonds's words: *If Henry Tudor had you in his hands, that clumsed head of yours would be chopped off before you could take another breath.*

Even so, I could make no resistance.

THIRTY-EIGHT

IT WOULD BE any number of days before I saw King Henry. At various times, I had my hands tied behind my back. I was blindfolded. I was locked in dark rooms. I was taken on horseback for many miles, but in which direction, or where, I didn't know. I was treated roughly, though at other times with respect. I was kept in a cell, a cell not so different from the one to which Brother Simonds had first taken me. I was sure I was going to be executed but had no idea when that might happen. I tried to pray. The best I could do was press my hands together and murmur, "Please."

Full of dread, I tried not to think of death. I tried to think of God. I found myself too dazed to have clear thoughts. The slightest sound startled me, made me think I was about to be taken, and that in turn made my heart pound so it grew sore.

After some long days, I believe it was an early evening, the door to the dark room in which I lay suddenly opened. A man whom I had never seen before appeared. His fine clothing told me he was a man of the court.

"Get up," came the order. "You're wanted."

"By whom?"

"King Henry."

My breath coming in quick, shallow gasps, I got up and tried to control my fright. I was led along many hallways, and while I caught glimpses of the outside, I had not the smallest idea as to where I was, other than in some great palace.

A door was opened. I was pushed inside a room. I heard the door shut behind me.

It was a large and mostly empty place, the only light coming from torches on the walls. Such light as there was seemed to quiver. The room had no furniture save for at the far end, where there was a throne-like chair. Seated in the chair was a man I had never seen before.

He was not a big man, but rather slight, with thin, reddish hair that hung down the back of his neck. His cheekbones were high, his face pale, and his lips thin, without emotion. His nose was somewhat large, while his small blue eyes, half lidded under thin eyebrows, fixed on me. I had the feeling that he was looking out from behind a mask.

His garments were simple, a deep purple robe with full sleeves. Small hands gripped the armrests as if he had a need to steady himself. On his head was a crown. I could see that it was real.

My heart filled with terror as I realized that this was King Henry.

"Come forward," he said firmly.

I managed, if only barely, to walk toward him, then collapsed upon my knees, my hands lifted in a prayerful supplication. Afraid to look on him, I bowed my head.

Into the silence, I whispered, "Mercy, great lord."

He did not speak. I kept my eyes cast down.

"What is your name?" he finally asked.

"Lambert Simnel."

"Who is your father?"

"I don't know."

"Mother?"

"No idea."

"An orphan?"

"Yes, my lord."

"How old are you?"

"I'm not sure."

"How did you come to claim to be Edward, Earl of Warwick?"

"A priest, Brother Richard Simonds, said that I was."

"Who employed him to do so?"

"The Earl of Lincoln."

"Where did the priest find you?"

"In Oxford. I was a scullion at Tackley's Tavern."

"Do you, in fact, have any claim to this crown?"

I finally looked up. "None, my lord. I only did as I was told."

He lifted his hands, pressed them together, and rested his fingertips on his mouth, all the while looking steadily at me with intense blue eyes.

"You say, boy, that you have no claim to the English throne. You are right. You do not."

For a long time he stared at me. I could only wonder what would happen.

He said, "If you repeat what I am about to say to anyone, your life will be over. Instantly. Pay heed.

"I took the crown from King Richard upon a battle field," he said. "I hardly have a better claim to kingship than you do. You might say I was a player king. The difference is, I won. You lost.

"I could take your life, and no one would say I did anything wrong."

He paused. I waited.

"You say you were a scullion. Is that right?"

"Yes, my lord."

"You are young and have been ill-used, so I intend to spare your life as long as you don't ever repeat what I just told you. As for now, I'll send you to my kitchen. There you may be a scullion. For me. Have you anything to say?"

What else could I do other than bow and say, "My lord, I'll do as I am told."

THIRTY-NINE

SO IT WAS. I returned to my kitchen work, this time in the palace of Westminster. My task is to slather mutton with new butter, dredge the chunks with salt and flour, spear them on a spit, and constantly turn that spit so as to roast the meat. While spinning the spit, I have to catch hot fat in the dripping pan, baste the mutton with those sizzling sauces, and know the moment it will melt—to be sure, not in *my* mouth but my master's.

That master is Henry Tudor, better known as Henry the Seventh, King of England.

What about Edward, the *real* Edward? As I would learn, there truly was a young Earl of Warwick. A simple boy. Henry had him in the Tower and kept him there. In November 1499, after a secret trial for treason, he was executed.

And I?

To be truthful, I sometimes recall how, for a brief moment, as if in the silence *between* the tolling of bells, the passing bells of my life, I was the king of England. Perhaps I was, though I am the only one who thinks of it. Once so low. Once so high. Now low again. Truly, wondrous things happened to me.

Had I been a simpleton to believe it all? Or had greatness been taken from me? How could I, in such a small splinter of time, a mere boy, have been so altered, and altered again, turned and turned yet again? What had it made of me?

When trying to understand it, I beg you to know that every now and again, in moments of aloneness, the thought does enter my head: *Who am I?*

I know the answer. I am Lambert Simnel, who was, once, very briefly, a king. The player king.

Be assured: All I have written here is true. I have a solitary groat to prove it. My name—Edward the Sixth—is on it.

But it will buy nothing.

AUTHOR'S NOTE

LAMBERT SIMNEL was a real person.

What unfolds in this book is based on what happened to him in England in the fifteenth century. A boy of uncertain age and name came out of nowhere; claimed to be the Earl of Warwick; was crowned King Edward the Sixth of England in Dublin, Ireland; led an invading army into England; and was defeated at the Battle of Stoke, only to become a scullion in the palace kitchen of King Henry the Seventh, the founder of the Tudor dynasty. There is some suggestion that Lambert later rose in position to become Henry's falconer.

Yet Simnel was and remains very much a mystery. Almost nothing about him is known, though the people who surrounded him—Brother Richard Simonds, the Earl of Lincoln, Francis Lovell, the soldier Martin Schwartz, even the tall Lord Darcy of Platen who carried him about Dublin on his shoulders—were real and are part of the historical record.

The friar, Richard Simonds (that may or may not have been his real name), was the man accused of teaching Lambert to be the Earl of Warwick.

Readers might like to know that the manners that Lambert was required to learn are not of my invention but come from the fifteenth-century work *Babees' Book*.

Likewise, there really was a Tackley's Tavern, which may, today, be visited along the High Street in Oxford, England. Be careful of the steps. They are steep.

There is no account as to what happened to Viscount Lovell save that he was last seen fleeing the Battle of Stoke in his armor. All that is known is that he disappeared.

However, his ancestral home was Minster Lovell,

and it was still standing two hundred years after the Battle of Stoke. In 1708, when building work was being carried out there, workers discovered a secret underground vault. When they opened it, they found the skeleton of a man seated at a table surrounded by writing materials and a book. People believed it was Lovell. Alas, when air was let into the chamber, the skeleton and the papers crumbled to dust.

Some believe Lovell's ghost haunts the area, a ghost in armor, riding a horse.

That, however, is another story.

A READING GROUP GUIDE TO

THE PLAYER
KING

BY AVI

❧ DISCUSSION QUESTIONS ❦

1. Historical fiction is a unique genre. There are some stories that take place in a real time period but with made up characters; other stories have real characters in real settings, but with made up dialogue; still others have historical context but no historical facts; some stories combine all those elements. What kind of historical fiction is this?

2. How does Lambert feel when he realizes what he has been chosen to do? Does this change how he feels about himself? Why or why not?

3. How does this experience change Lambert's life? How does it change his relationship to those around him? How does the direct order, "Do as you're told," add to this experience?

4. Lambert tries to run away several times, and then chooses not to try anymore. What happened that changed his mind? Why did he want to run away? What would you have done if you were in his shoes?

5. How does Brother Simonds treat Lambert? How does their relationship change over the course of the story?

6. Who are Lambert's friends? Does he have any?

7. Lambert's rise and fall is based on a lie. What events cause Lambert to follow along? What are the consequences of this lie?

8. How does this experience change Lambert's relationship to others? Do his newfound knowledge, ability to read and write, and manners make things easier or harder for him? In your opinion, is knowledge a good thing or a dangerous thing?

9. In Chapter 38, Lambert and King Henry VII have a conversation where King Henry suggests that there are no real differences between the two of them. Do you agree or disagree with this? What is the motivation behind the conversation? What does this tell us about King Henry?

10. How does Lambert change from the beginning of the novel to the end?